Hosta la Vista

Isabella Proctor Cozy Mysteries

Book 9

Lisa Bouchard

Lisa Bouchard

Copyright 2023 by Lisa Bouchard

All rights reserved.

No part of this book may be reproduced, scanned, transmitted, or distributed in any printed or electronic form by any means, including photocopying, recording, or other electronic or mechanical methods, without the prior written permission of Lisa Bouchard, except in the case of brief quotations embodied within reviews and other non-commercial uses allowed by copyright law.

> For permission requests, email
> Lisa@LisaBouchard.com
> www.LisaBouchard.com

This is a work of fiction. Names, characters, places, and incidents either are the product of the author's imagination or are used fictitiously, and any resemblance to actual persons, living or dead, business establishments, events, or locales is entirely coincidental.

Lisa Bouchard

For Paul, who supports all my dreams.

Table of Contents

Chapter 1 1
Chapter 2 13
Chapter 3 25
Chapter 4 36
Chapter 5 52
Chapter 6 67
Chapter 7 77
Chapter 8 88
Chapter 9 102
Chapter 10 112
Chapter 11 125
Chapter 12 137
Chapter 13 151
Chapter 14 166
Chapter 15 178
Chapter 16 188
Chapter 17 201
Chapter 18 211
Chapter 19 225
Chapter 20 240
Chapter 21 257

Special Acknowledgements 272
But wait, there's more! 274

Chapter 1

What was the old saying? Lucky in cards, unlucky in love?

Maybe I should hit up a casino, because love wasn't working out for me. Come to think about it, almost everything wasn't working out for me right now.

Mackenzie had quit to move to Canada. Jameson was tired of me breaking eggs in teleportation practice and had told me to go back to practicing with pennies. Customers weren't coming in as often as they had been, and the money I'd saved to expand the business was going to keep the lights on.

And Palmer hadn't called me. Not once in four weeks. I suppose that was what happened when a couple broke up, but I'd gotten so used to working with him on cases that life seemed boring and dull. I worried too. What if he ran into a paranormal case but didn't realize it until it was too late?

The apothecary door chimes rang. My mother walked in with my aunts in tow. And they took their spring coats off, so they were going to stay a while. This couldn't be good. Generally speaking, they didn't come to the apothecary unless something was wrong. All three of them here at once was a very bad sign. I stood and walked around the counter I'd been sitting at for the last hour. "What is it? Is something wrong with Grandma?"

"Your grandmother is fine," my mother said. "It's you we're worried about."

I pasted a fake grin onto my face. "Me? Why? It's been weeks and I'm completely over him. If he can't take a woman doing the same job he does, then he's not the man for me."

Aunt Nadia frowned. "So you've said. Repeatedly, but you're not fooling anyone."

Aunt Lily looked concerned. "The fact that you know what we're talking about says you're not over him yet."

I knew that, but I was comfortable with the polite fiction that everything was fine. Sooner or later, I'd stop missing him and life would go on as normal. "What gave me away?"

"Jameson. He's worried enough about you that he came to talk to us."

Great. Now my cat was getting involved in my love life. He must have been exceptionally worried, though, because it took a great deal of energy for a familiar to talk to anyone who wasn't his witch. "And did he have any solutions?"

Aunt Lily snorted a laugh. "Yes, but you'd never agree to them, and I doubt they'd even work."

I leaned back against the counter. "Like what?"

"His first idea was to teleport you and Steven to a deserted island and leave you there for weeks. He'd check in on you and make sure you weren't starving, but he wouldn't bring you back home until you'd worked out your differences," Aunt Nadia said.

Yeah, that wouldn't work. We were both too stubborn to let a blatant manipulation change our minds. "Anything a little more reasonable?"

"Not really. He didn't realize arranged marriages didn't happen anymore. After that, he decided it was a human problem and told us to work it out," my mother said.

"Work it out? How on earth could the three of you work it out?" I asked. Before anyone answered, I continued. "Never mind. I don't want to know. I don't want to think about him, or my love life at all." I looked at each of the aunts. They had to be here for a reason, and not just to deliver a message from my cat, who I lived with and spoke to every day. "What's the real reason you're here?"

They stepped closer to me and enveloped me in a hug. I hadn't had a group aunts' hug in a long time, and it felt good having their love directed at me in such a palpable way. They stepped back and my mother said, "Don't get angry."

My heart sank. If there was ever a time to get angry, it was probably when someone told you not to. "What did you do?"

"I know it didn't work out so well last time, but I've got a much better idea now of what kind of person you want to date, so I've set you up with a very nice young—"

"No," I said flatly.

My mother continued. "A very nice young man. He's a witch, Christina's grandson, and I think you'll like him."

What was it about mothers setting up their daughters on dates? My birthday was soon, but I was only twenty-one. I still had six more years to find a husband, get married, and have children. If I wanted to get married—not everyone did these days. And if I wanted to have children. Plenty of women were skipping both marriage and children, and the more I thought about it, the better it sounded.

"Christina is very excited about this date. She also thinks the two of you would make a great couple," Aunt Lily said.

I squeezed my eyes shut. I was going to have to go on this date, if only to keep the sorority happy. We'd finally gotten to a decent working relationship after their disappointment about some of the familiars moving to California. Rejecting Christina's grandson without giving him a chance might make the situation difficult. Also, I could play this to my advantage. I opened my eyes. "Fine. But I have conditions."

"Understandable," Aunt Nadia said.

"One date, here in Portsmouth. No promise of a second date, or that I'll ever speak to him again. And no setting me up with anyone ever again."

My mother frowned. "But what if I find someone who's perfect for you?"

I sighed. "If he's perfect for me, we'll find each other."

The aunts smiled at having got what they wanted. I was sure they thought they'd be able to talk their way around my conditions in the future, but they were underestimating how stubborn I'd be on this topic.

"The shop looks so nice," Aunt Nadia said. "I like what you've done with the candle display."

It wasn't as tidy as when Mackenzie was still here, but it was still clean enough. The candle display hadn't changed for a year, but I appreciated the compliment. "Thanks, Aunt Nadia. Do you set Delia up on dates like this? I don't recall her complaining about it."

Aunt Nadia shook her head. "Oh, no. I tried to set her up on a date once, and she didn't let me hear the end of it for weeks. It's not worth the anguish. And Lily had to dodge spells being flung at her when she tried to set Thea up with someone."

I licked my lips. "So what you're saying is that being nice doesn't pay? Okay—lesson learned. This will be the last date you ever set me up on."

They started walking toward the door. "And with the help of the goddess, it will be the last time we'll ever need to," my mother said.

After they left, I grabbed the broom and started sweeping. There was no reason I couldn't keep the apothecary tidier. I tried to remember if Christina had ever spoken about her family before, but nothing came to mind. I should have asked what his name was, but I hadn't actually cared that much. Whoever this poor guy was, he was my ticket to never being set up again.

I worked in the prep room all afternoon, experimenting with new spring products, hoping to entice my customers back into the shop. At five o'clock my phone rang, and the caller ID told me it was Liam Nyquist calling. I didn't know anyone with that name, so I steeled myself for an awkward conversation with my blind date.

"Hello, this is Isabella," I said in a cheerier tone than I felt.

"Hi. Uh . . . my name is Liam, and my grandmother gave me your number."

Oh goddess, he sounded young. I was so enthusiastic about putting an end to any future blind dates that it hadn't mattered to me at the time. Now I was worried, because I thought his voice cracked. "Hi, Liam. It's embarrassing what our families will put us through, isn't it?"

He chuckled. "It is. You know my Grandma Chrissy, and it's almost impossible to tell her no."

Grandma Chrissy? She was so serious in all our sorority meetings that I had a hard time imagining she let anyone call her by a nickname. "You're right about that. My family is the same."

"Are you busy tomorrow night? I thought maybe we could have a low-key date, just a walk downtown or through the park. No pressure."

I liked the sound of that. "If the weather holds out, that sounds good. I'll be at work until six, so we'll have almost an hour of sunlight. I work in the middle of town, so why don't you meet me at the apothecary?"

"Six o'clock tomorrow, then," he said. "I'm looking forward to it."

We hung up and I wasn't sure what to think. I picked up the vial I'd been heating ingredients in and swirled it. Maybe I'd imagined he sounded too young for me. He sounded younger than Palmer, but I was not going to compare the two men. No way. Just because I was beginning to think Palmer and I might have built a life together, that didn't mean any other person I dated had to be better than he was.

In fact, Liam had a few points in his favor. I didn't have to explain magic or the sorority to him. He already knew I did dangerous things sometimes and couldn't claim to be surprised if I came home a little banged up. I nodded to myself. This could work out.

But then I thought about Christina. What had she told him about me? She and I hadn't started out as friends when I joined the sorority, and I'd had to work hard to earn her respect. Some days, I still wasn't sure I had. He seemed interested in meeting me, so she couldn't have told him much that was bad.

I put the vial of goldenrod and lilac back over the small gas flame and heated it. This date was beginning to feel more important to me than I'd been willing to admit, but obsessing over it wouldn't do me any good.

Chapter 2

There had been a lot of important days in my life, but the day I had my date with Liam was the day that changed my life. I didn't know it at the time though.

With Mackenzie gone, I had to buy my own pastry and coffee each morning. As I walked to the Fancy Tart, I resolved to start looking for someone to take her place that day. Closer to downtown, the smell of burning plastic and wood on the wet spring air caught my attention. It wasn't until I turned the corner onto Market

Street that I saw what had burned. The Fancy Tart.

Smoke streamed out the broken front windows. Fire and police vehicles surrounded the building, and a crowd of gawkers watched the firefighters' every move. I froze for a second, hardly able to believe what I was seeing.

I sprinted down the block and frantically looked for someone I knew. Kate was directing traffic around the road blocked by emergency vehicles, and Papatonis was making sure no one entered the cordoned-off area. He might know what had happened and who, if anyone, had been hurt.

"What happened?" I asked him, panting from the short sprint.

"Pretty much what you see here. The building's burned down," he replied.

Not very helpful, and I wondered if he was being abrupt with me because Palmer and I had broken up. "I used to work here. Was anyone in the fire? Is anyone hurt?"

He shifted from foot to foot, then looked behind him. "Listen, if Palmer sees me talking to you about a case, he'll have my hide."

I gave him a pleading look and didn't bother to hide the tears welling in my eyes.

He looked behind him again to Palmer, who was facing away from us. "The fire's been out for about ten minutes, and they're still looking through the building. We don't know the cause of the fire. If it means anything, I hope none of your friends were in there. Now could you please go before he sees me talking to you?"

"Thanks." I walked away, following the cordon toward the building. I could sneak in using any number of magic spells and see what was going on for myself but, if something happened and I was hurt, I might not be able to drop the spell. I shuddered, remembering the cloaking spell I'd used as a child before I knew how to reverse it. And if Palmer caught me investigating in a dangerous area, he'd know he made the right choice to break up with me.

I stood there, straining to see anything happening inside, letting tears run down my face. Eventually, Kate joined me.

"You okay?" she asked.

I took a deep breath. "No. I used to work here. The owner's a friend of mine." As I said this, I realized I hadn't seen Bethany. The police would have called her to come down by now.

"I've got to get back to work, but I wanted to say just because you and Palmer called it quits, doesn't mean we can't still be friends, right?"

I looked away from the burned building to my friend. "Right. Did someone call the owner? Is she here?"

"It's standard procedure. I'm sure someone got hold of her."

"It's just . . . I don't see her here, and I'm worried."

Kate pressed the button on her radio. "Has the owner shown up yet?"

Palmer's voice answered. "No. She didn't answer her phone." He turned, scanning the crowd. When he found Kate and me, he scowled. "Kate! Back to work."

She gave me a quick hug. "Got to get back. I'll call you sometime soon."

Palmer continued to glare at me. I stared back at him. He wasn't going to use his angry cop face to make me leave. I could stand here all day if I wanted to. He didn't look away until a firefighter started talking to him.

I looked away and examined the building. There was very little damage to the buildings on either side of the bakery. I didn't know anything about fires or how to tell if one was arson or not, but this looked suspicious to me.

Palmer cleared his throat and startled me. I had been looking at the burned building so intently, I hadn't realized he'd joined me. "You should go."

I gave him my frostiest stare. "I don't think so. I want to be here when Bethany arrives."

He closed his eyes for a moment. "Please, for once, just do as you're told."

I didn't know why he thought that would work on me. He and Grandma had commiserated often enough to know I rarely did what anyone told me. "I'll go when the rest of the spectators go."

He rubbed his face with his hands. "The coroner will be here any minute now, and I didn't want you to see that. But hey, if you're not going to take my advice and leave, fine. I warned you, and I can't keep worrying about you like this."

He turned and walked away before I could say anything. The nerve! He couldn't worry about me? The whole reason I'd insisted on being brought in on cases was to protect him. Worrying went both ways, but I was the only one who could protect from both magic and non-magic threats.

Lucy got out of the coroner's van with her assistant. They retrieved a gurney from the back and checked in with one of the firefighters, who led them into the building. I pulled out my phone and called Bethany. Her phone went straight to voice mail, and I wondered if it had been destroyed in the fire. Next I called Omar.

"Yeah?" a groggy voice answered.

"Hey, Omar. It's Isabella." I gave him a moment to wake up before I continued. "I'm at the bakery, and there's been a fire."

"What? Is everyone okay?" he asked.

I sighed. "I don't think so. The coroner just went in. I tried calling Bethany, but she didn't pick up."

"Don't go anywhere, I'll be right there."

I looked at the time on my phone. I still had an hour before I had to open the apothecary. I was tempted to follow Lucy into the building, under a cloaking spell, but Omar would be looking for me in a couple minutes. Instead, I focused on the remaining firefighters and police, trying to read their lips and figure out what was going on.

I needed Jameson to teach me a spell to hear people when they were far away, because I couldn't make out what anyone was saying.

I saw Omar striding toward me and waved. He waved back, and I walked to meet him. I waited by the coroner's van so I could ask Lucy a question before she left.

"Do you know who was working this morning?" I asked.

"It might have just been Bethany. Andrew's been out sick for a few days," Omar said.

My hopes for Bethany were vanishing. If Andrew had the day off, then she would have been in early to do the baking. There was a very good chance that the body they brought out would be hers. My stomach clenched, afraid of what I would see. I couldn't look away, though. I had to know if it was Bethany.

Omar put his arm around my shoulder. "We don't know anything yet, let's not panic."

I looked to the building then back to Omar. The small crowd that had gathered gasped as I heard the wheels of the coroner's gurney. They were bringing out a body. I turned to look as Palmer unzipped the body bag. His grim expression made my knees buckle.

"Hey, hang on there," Omar said. "Let's find you somewhere to sit."

He moved his arm to support me around the waist. He walked me across the street and leaned me against the Irish knitwear store's wall. "I'll ask who they found. You wait here," he said.

I slid down the wall until I was sitting on the sidewalk. Bethany didn't deserve to have her building burned down. I watched Omar cross the street to speak to Palmer. Palmer shook his head but when Omar pointed to me, Palmer said something. They both joined me, and Palmer crouched down to be at my eye level.

"You have both worked at the bakery for a long time. Do you feel up to identifying the body?"

No. Absolutely not. I did not want to look at another lifeless body of a friend or acquaintance.

"I'll go," Omar said.

"The sooner the victim is identified, the sooner we can focus our investigation," Palmer said softly.

I choked back a sob and looked away from him. I needed the Palmer that cared about me, but he was all business, not even giving my hand a quick squeeze. "Thank you for letting me know."

Palmer stood and the two men left me on the sidewalk. Palmer led Omar into the coroner's van. I stood so I could see Omar better, and I caught a flash of Bethany's blonde hair. Omar nodded and his face went pale.

I walked across the street to Omar and Palmer.

"It's her," Omar whispered.

I took his hand in mine. "I know. Are you okay?"

He took a shuddering breath. "I will be."

Palmer turned to Omar. "I'd like to talk to you about Mrs. Swift. Can I give you a lift home?"

I looked from Omar to Palmer. Palmer wasn't looking at me. Was he avoiding me as best as he could? And did he suspect Omar was involved in the fire? Other than an interrogation room, there was no better place to ask people questions than while you were in a car together. The awkward silence that comes after a question has most people rushing to speak.

"I'll come with you," I said, in case Palmer was trying to question Omar.

"No. That's not necessary. I may need to question you later, so don't leave town without telling me first."

My eyes widened. Don't leave town? Was I a suspect too? "I won't, Detective. But if you can't locate me, my family always knows where I am."

I tried not to scowl at him, but I was pretty sure I failed. "Thank you, Miss Proctor."

Oh goddess, I was in trouble. If we were back to Detective and Miss Proctor, then he must have known something I didn't—something that made me look guilty.

Chapter 3

I made my way to the apothecary, walking slowly and trying not to think about what had happened to Bethany. I looked in store windows decorated with spring flowers as if they could urge the warm days of late spring to arrive sooner. My hands shook as I unlocked the wooden apothecary door. I closed it behind me and, even though it was close to opening time, I didn't change the sign to say open. I needed a few minutes before I could speak with other people.

I sat at my desk and put my head down. Who would want to kill Bethany? She made pastry and sold coffee. She wasn't a difficult boss to work for, as long as you did everything her way, and she'd never hinted at any problems in her personal life. I sighed and lifted my head. My brain went straight to murder when this could have easily been nothing but a horrible accident. A short in the electrical equipment, or an oven accidentally left on overnight.

The sorority hadn't had much to deal with over the past month, and I hadn't been called in to work a case with Palmer since we broke up, so I didn't need to look at every dead person and wonder who had killed them. The truth was, most people died by accident or natural causes and not because someone was out to get them—magical or not.

I went back out to the shop and started my opening routine. As I lit Trina's candle, a new wave of sadness hit me. She'd been gone for a little over a year now, and I still missed her. "Bethany died this morning," I told the flame. "I feel like I'm on my own with the apothecary now." Bethany had stepped in to help me when I first took over, and her guidance kept me from making some costly mistakes. I hadn't needed her advice for more than a month or two, but it was comforting knowing I had someone who could help me work out any issues I ran into with the shop.

Today's tea needed to be strong. I took the lapsang souchong for the caffeinated tea. In Bethany's honor, I took down the roasted chicory root from the herb wall for today's decaf tea. Its nutty flavor reminded me of hazelnut coffee. I poured myself a cup of the lapsang souchong and looked around the shop. It needed a quick sweep, and a few items on shelves needed to be straightened. Mackenzie wouldn't have left the shop until it was perfectly set up for the next day, and I missed her perfectionist touches. When I had a lull in customers, I'd run a new ad looking for help.

I switched the sign on the door and prepared to greet the day's customers.

By four o'clock I was exhausted. It seemed that everyone wanted to talk about Bethany, the bakery, and whether it would be rebuilt or not. Mrs. Williams wondered if Bethany's brother Andrew would take over for her. He'd worked there for decades and knew everything about running a bakery.

Mr. Wilcox said I should buy the bakery to expand my businesses. He said it wasn't good to have all my eggs in one basket. He was right, but I wasn't ready for a new set of responsibilities, and I might never be. Not unless the sorority put themselves out of business by apprehending every member of the fraternity. That wasn't likely to happen any time soon.

My phone rang. I didn't recognize the number, but it could be Liam, so I didn't let it go to voice mail. "Good afternoon. Is this Isabella?"

Oh bats, it was him. I really didn't want to go out on a date tonight, but I didn't want to spend the night with family or alone either. "Oh, Liam, hi. About tonight—"

"Oh good," he rushed in. "I was worried you'd forget. I thought we could keep it low-key and maybe just go for a walk."

He sounded so enthusiastic that I hated to turn him down. "I need to have an early night, but a walk sounds good."

I could practically hear his grin through the phone. "I'll pick you up at six, at the apothecary. See you then."

We hung up and I looked down at my outfit. The jeans had seen better days, and my thrift store sweater tended to stretch out by the end of the day. I had to learn the tailoring spell Delia used to make Thea and me outfits for the conference we went to in Boston. For tonight, I'd have to wear the emergency outfit I kept in the office.

Why an emergency outfit? Some days potion making didn't work so well and I'd be covered in leaves, rubbing alcohol, or any number of other potion ingredients. Trina trained me from the beginning to avoid using magic where customers might see me, so I never used magic to refresh my outfit.

Before I could change, my phone rang again and Chief Dobbins's face appeared on the screen. I hadn't spoken to him in quite a while and couldn't imagine what he wanted. "Good afternoon, Chief. How can I help you?"

He cleared his throat. "Good afternoon. I'd like you to come in and consult on a case."

My stomach clenched. Even if he didn't want me to work on one of Palmer's cases, I'd see him around. After how he reacted to me this morning, I thought it would be good to stay out of each other's way. "Are you sure? You know Palmer and I broke up, right?"

"I know, and it's a darn shame because you two were good together. I want you on the Fancy Tart case. Palmer said he can work with you and keep it professional. Can you do the same?"

Now that was a good question. Tonight's date showed I was moving on from him, so maybe I could. And I wanted to know what happened to Bethany. If I wasn't on the case, I might never hear the full story. On the other hand, the scene didn't have any obvious signs of magic. "So it wasn't an accident? Why do you need me? And wouldn't the fire inspector be in charge of the investigation?"

He sighed. "Fire investigators are working on the arson aspect, and you and Palmer will be working on the murder. She was dead before the building caught fire. As for the other thing, none of the adjacent buildings were damaged, and I have a hunch this case needs your expertise. Besides, you and Palmer make an excellent team. He's not the same without you."

Was he using witch mother guilt on me? I did not need that, not with a grandmother, a mother, and two aunts who were masters in the field. "Let me see if I can find someone to help out in the shop tomorrow. If I can, I'll give you a call."

I changed into my emergency outfit and sat at my desk. Rather than write up a new ad like I had planned to, I ran the same ad I'd used to find Mackenzie. The ad wouldn't fix my tomorrow problem, so I called my mother. "What are your plans for tomorrow?" I asked.

"Not much, I was going to plan for Ostara, but I can do that any time. What do you need?"

I sighed. "I guess what I need first is advice."

She said, "I'll be right there," then hung up. In one moment, she appeared in front of me.

She sat in the upholstered wingback visitor's chair. "You sounded upset. What's up?"

I leaned back and closed my eyes. "The chief called and wants me to work with Palmer on the Fancy Tart case."

Her eyes widened. "We heard it burned. Was anyone in the building?"

I'd hoped she already knew so I didn't have to say the words. I nodded. "Bethany. The coroner has her now."

In an instant, she was hugging me. "I'm so sorry. I know how much she meant to you. What do you need?"

"I need you to watch the shop tomorrow. Maybe longer. I'm working on hiring someone to replace Mackenzie, but I can't guarantee I'll find someone soon."

She kissed my forehead then straightened. "Of course. What makes Ray think she was killed with magic?"

I frowned. "He said he's got a hunch, but I'm not sure. I was going to take Jameson over so we could check for magic once I can bring myself to go in. I think Chief's also trying to maneuver Palmer and me back together."

My mother laughed. "Who'd have thought Ray Dobbins would play matchmaker?"

I grinned. He was as unlikely a matchmaker as you could get. He was a short, bald man, but the sadness he'd always had in his eyes was going away. Maybe his renewed friendship with Aunt Lily had him thinking more about romance. "I saw Palmer at the fire today. He wasn't happy I was there, but he asked Omar to identify the body." I took a deep breath. "I only saw her hair, but I knew it was her."

"I'm so sorry. She was a lovely woman."

She was, and I wasn't sure how I would get along without her. I handed my mother the spare set of keys to the shop. "There's nothing special going on tomorrow, so just open the shop at ten and close it at six. Liam will be here any minute now to pick me up for our date."

"Don't you worry about a thing. I'll call you after six tomorrow and let you know how it all went. And if you need me for longer, that's not a problem."

For as difficult as family can be sometimes, it was nice to know I could count on them when I needed to.

Chapter 4

I ran through my closing routine quickly, saving Trina's candle for last. "I've got a date tonight and, even though it's just a casual walk, I'm not sure it's the right thing for me." As usual, the candle didn't tell me anything, but I still felt like someone had heard my problems.

Liam arrived promptly at six. He had the same high cheekbones as his grandmother, but his brown eyes had a lot more cheer in them. His short brown hair had a little curl to it that he wasn't successful in smoothing out. He was about five inches taller than me and wasn't in as good shape as my last blind date. That wasn't a problem, given the odd dietary manipulations Geoff had to live with.

I held my hand out to him. "Hi, I'm Isabella."

His hand was warm when he shook mine. "I'm Liam. It's nice to meet you, and thank you for agreeing to this date. My grandma won't let up on me about finding a nice young witch to settle down with. I think she's set me up with just about every eligible witch in New England."

I smiled at him. He just told me I was the one of the last possible choices Christina would make, but I didn't think he realized he was insulting me. "It's good to meet you too."

He looked around. "Is this your shop? What do you sell?"

I was still smiling. It was nice to be with a man I didn't have to hide any parts of myself from. I thought I didn't have to hide myself from Palmer, but our breakup proved otherwise. "I've got tea, candles, and a few other non-magical items. I sell a lot of potions for low-level illness or aches and pains. I also have a great set of products designed to bring harmony into the home. Those are the things I'm proudest of."

His eyes widened. "Potions, wow. I've always found them very difficult and, when I was learning, it was not a good idea to use my potions unless you checked them out carefully first."

I laughed. "I'm no good with . . ." Since I'd gotten my amulet, there wasn't a lot I couldn't do. Anything I wasn't good at, Jameson trained me in until I was. "With feeling whether magic had been used recently."

Liam rolled his eyes. "Grandma Chrissy is very good at that. She could always tell if I'd used magic when I shouldn't have as a kid."

The aunts could tell when we'd used magic as kids, too, but I thought they were probably kinder than Christina when they caught us. "Should we go?" I asked.

He nodded and we left. I locked the door and refreshed the wards. With Alex keeping watch on the apothecary from his tent in the courtyard, I was confident no one would try to break in, but no witch worth her spells lets her wards lose their strength. "If you don't mind, I don't want to walk down Market Street. There was a fire and . . ."

"We can go wherever you want. You pick our route," Liam said.

I led him down Islington Street, trying not to feel weird about being out with a man who wasn't Palmer. "What do you do for work?" I asked.

"I'm a forester."

I stumbled, thinking he said Forster. I readied a cloaking spell but didn't release it.

"I work for the state, managing the state parks, making sure the forests are healthy and no trees are in danger of falling on hikers."

I let out my breath and dropped the spell. "Interesting. So you work with plants too."

He nodded and we continued walking toward the Portsmouth Public Library. "There's not a lot I can do with magic in my job, but I love being outdoors and working with my hands. How did you get into the apothecary business?"

It had been a year, and I was better at explaining my inheritance without breaking into tears. "I inherited it from my mentor, the former owner."

He reached out and squeezed my hand. "Tough way to start out."

"It was. And when she died I was also working at the Fancy Tart."

He didn't recognize the name, so I continued. "The bakery that burned down early this morning."

This time he stopped walking. "I'm so sorry. You probably had friends who worked there. At least it was early in the morning, right?"

I shook my head and willed myself not to cry. "The owner was there and she didn't make it out."

He looked genuinely sad for me. "Do you know what happened?"

I released his hand and wrapped my arm around his. Palmer would be furious if I gave out any information about the case. "No. The police haven't got any leads yet, as far as I know." I started walking again. "If you don't mind, I'd rather talk about something else."

"Of course. What are your plans for Ostara?"

My stomach growled and I hoped he hadn't heard it. "We always start the new annual seeds for the garden, and my Aunt Nadia makes a huge omelet for dinner. We keep it fairly simple now that there aren't any kids in the house. How about you?"

"I'm spending the equinox in the woods. My brother and I will be camping and enjoying the early spring weather."

In theory, this sounded like a perfect celebration. "But hasn't it rained for the last eight Ostara nights in a row? You must have the same enchanted tents we used as kids."

"We had them when we were young, too, but I prefer to experience the change of the seasons without magic," he said.

"It's also my birthday soon, so I'm sure there will be some surprise planned for me."

"Happy birthday! May the goddess bring you a happy and healthy year."

I was really beginning to like this guy. Was it possible the aunts had finally found someone suitable for me? He was so open and happy, unlike Palmer who was serious most of the time. The difference in Liam's and Palmer's jobs explained a lot. If Palmer could spend his days communing with nature instead of hunting down murderers, he'd have a much sunnier attitude, too.

My stomach growled again. I hadn't eaten much for lunch and had nothing but tea for breakfast.

"I know we said we'd just go for a walk, but can I buy you something to eat? We don't need to go to a restaurant, but your body is clearly telling you that you need food."

"Dinner sounds fantastic. I haven't eaten much today—too much upheaval and stress—and now I'm starving. Do you like Indian food?"

"If the goddess didn't create aloo gobi herself, I'd be surprised. Lead the way."

We walked the four blocks to my favorite Indian restaurant, Shalimar, talking about our childhoods and what our parents did to keep us out of magical trouble. It was cold enough that we didn't need to worry about strangers on the street listening to us—everyone was walking quickly to get to their destination. I smiled at the vibrant mandalas painted on the side of the restaurant when they came into view. And my date ate carbs. The night was looking up.

Unsurprisingly, Liam ordered aloo gobi while I ordered sag paneer and samosas for us to share. "Are you a vegetarian?" I asked.

"Not completely, but I only eat meat a few times a week. Why? Are you?"

I shook my head. "Not even a little, but that doesn't mean I don't enjoy a meal without meat."

The waiter returned with our food and, before I could start eating, Liam caught my hand and held it. "I hope I'm not being too forward, but I think this is going well."

I smiled, about to tell him I was having a much better time with him than I had any right to expect out of a blind date, when I saw Palmer standing at the hostess station. I quashed the reflex to pull my hand out of Liam's.

He turned to follow my gaze. "Who's that?"

"My ex," I said in a loud whisper.

Palmer couldn't possibly have heard me, but he turned to look at us anyway. He looked from me, to Liam, to our hands in the middle of the table. I wanted to sink down and let the tablecloth hide me, but it was too late. He was walking toward us.

He loomed over us. "Good evening, Miss Proctor."

"Detective. What are you doing here?" I asked.

"I'm getting a quick dinner before I go back to work. I hear you're joining me on the bakery case. Make sure you're at the station by seven tomorrow morning."

"I will. I'm looking forward to solving this one."

Palmer looked back to our hands, then scowled at Liam. Liam released my hand and stood. "Liam Nyquist. Good to meet you, Detective."

Palmer took Liam's outstretched hand. "You too."

Palmer took his food from the hostess and strode out. Liam sat but didn't take my hand again. "That is one unhappy man."

"What makes you say that?" I asked.

"His microexpressions when he first saw us together. He's angry that you're out for dinner with another man. Sure, he covered the scowl up convincingly, but he couldn't hide what he was feeling."

I looked down at my rapidly cooling sag paneer. "Would you be upset if I said I wanted to go home?"

"Upset? No. Disappointed, of course. But I get it. It's been a horrible day for you, and running into your ex on your first date with another guy would put anyone over the edge. Even if they didn't have to work with them in the morning."

Goddess help me, Liam was starting to seem like the perfect guy. "Thanks."

"I'd like to drive you home though. I suspect that if he sees you going home on your own, he'd let me know how upset he was."

I smiled at him. This was a no-win situation. If Liam didn't give me a ride home, Palmer would be angry. But if I took a ride from a man I'd only met this evening, Palmer would be angry. It was a good thing neither of us lived for his opinion. "I'm not sure he would, but that doesn't mean he wouldn't think about it. And after today, a ride sounds terrific. Is your car nearby?"

He stood. "Yes. It's down the street in the municipal lot."

His car was a bright blue Chevy Bolt, and it looked like he'd just had it washed. By this time of the spring, most cars were filthy with the dirt and ice used to keep the roads clear. He opened the passenger door for me and I got in.

"All I need is your address," he said as he buckled his seatbelt. I gave him my apartment's address, and he relayed it to the map program on his phone.

I tried to think of fun or interesting things to talk about on the short drive, but my mind was swirling with thoughts of Bethany, Omar, and Palmer. It was a good thing the chief called me in on the case, because the more I thought about it, the more worried I got. What if it were a magical killing? Even though Palmer still had the protection amulet my family made him, it wouldn't protect him from the strongest witches or the worst spells.

Liam pulled into my parking lot and turned his car off. "I'd like to walk you to your door, if you don't mind."

I didn't mind. In fact, I was relieved. "Thanks. Bethany's death has me a little on edge."

"Of course it does. That's only natural. I'll walk you in, and you can check your apartment's wards. If nothing's gotten through them, we'll both know you're safe."

I led the way to my door, wondering how my mother could have set me up on so many horrible blind dates and how she finally got one right. It could be that even she got lucky once in a while.

At the top of the stairs, I whispered to him. "My neighbor, Bruce, is always listening for neighbors to complain to, and about."

He nodded as we crept silently along the hallway. As we reached Bruce's door, he pulled it open. "Aha! I thought I heard someone."

That was a load of guano. We'd been silent, and we even avoided the squeaky floorboard. I bet he had a camera set up somewhere, with some sort of motion detector alarm. How else would he be able to know when I got home as reliably as he did? "Good evening, Bruce. Have a good night."

I kept walking and he kept talking. "Wait a minute there. Why are you bringing another guy into your apartment?"

I rolled my eyes. "What are you talking about? And why do you think my life is any of your business?"

"I'm merely walking Miss Proctor to her door, then I'll be off to my own home. Don't let us keep you from your work."

"Uh, right. Just make sure you two don't make a lot of noise tonight. I've got a busy day tomorrow and need a good night's sleep."

Bruce closed his door and I gave Liam a small smile. "Guess I didn't win the neighbor lottery this time." I checked the wards on my door, and they were intact. I unlocked the door and turned to say goodnight to Liam. "Thank you for dinner. You made tonight as good as it could have been."

He beamed at me. "You're most welcome. I'd like to call you and maybe we can go out again, once you're not grieving for a friend."

"I'd like that," I said.

He turned and walked away, without even trying to kiss me. He was a nice enough guy that I wouldn't have minded. I heard Bruce's door close again a moment before I closed mine. He already knew who was in the hall, why did he have to look again? My neighbor was turning out to be a creepy stalker. I needed to talk to Mr. Subramanian about him.

"Jameson? I'm home."

He walked out of his bedroom, yawning. "It's about time. Who was that man at the door?"

I plopped down on the couch. "I had a date tonight with Christina's grandson Liam."

Jameson jumped up on the couch next to me. "A date? You didn't check that with me first."

I scowled. "No, I didn't. And I don't plan to start running my dates past you first to make sure you approve. Besides, my mother set us up. You know how that goes. Sooner or later she wins out, and I wind up going out with the guy. At least this one was nice. And normal."

Chapter 5

I wasn't bright-eyed and bushy-tailed, but I was at the police station before seven the next morning. Jameson didn't buy my argument that I was in mourning for my friend, and we practiced teleportation until I was so tired that just looking at a penny drove it into the coffee table.

I knew I was getting better—not that he'd acknowledge the fact. I fell into bed after the fastest evening routine I could manage and woke up two minutes after my alarm started ringing.

Officer Searle, the duty officer, walked me back to Palmer's desk. He had been injured in the line of duty and walked with a cane. He couldn't work cases but he took his job as seriously as anyone else in the building.

"He said there'd be a stack of files for you to read through. He wants you in the conference room."

There was a four-inch stack of files with my name written on a sticky note attached to the top folder. "These must be for me. Is he here? I'd like to check in with him before I start."

The sergeant, Sergeant Wohan, grinned. "No. He's not planning to be here until nine. Said he wanted to give you plenty of time to catch up before the two of you got started."

I tried not to roll my eyes, but I was still tired and my self-control wasn't very good. "Great. Thanks. I guess I'll see him when he gets here." I walked toward the conference room, eyeing Kate's desk as I walked by. It was cleaned off and ready for her day, whenever she got here.

The first file was labeled with Bethany's name. I sat and started reading. By the time I'd finished her file, I had a very different picture of the woman I thought I knew. She may have been a calm, quiet baker when I knew her, but she had a past that could rival Grandma's. If there was a cause, a march, or a demonstration to be had in the late sixties, she was involved. Often in the front lines. Consequently, her record was full of minor arrests for disturbing the peace, protesting without a permit, and vandalism.

I closed the folder, thinking that we were all strangers to each other to some extent. We all had secrets we didn't share.

Omar's file was next. I sighed and opened it. At least it was much thinner than Bethany's. Omar was a student at the University of New Hampshire, had large amounts of debt, and whoever had assembled the file had speculated that he might be susceptible to bribery. I shook my head. Omar had one low-limit credit card that was at half full and a staggering amount of student loans. He was a business major with a concentration in international finance. He'd find a way to pay back his loans.

I'd finished the third file, on Bethany's brother, by the time Palmer arrived. He pushed his way through the door, carrying another armload of files. "Miss Proctor."

So we were still going to be like that. "Detective Palmer. I'd like to talk to you about the analysis in Omar's file."

He raised an eyebrow but said nothing.

"Someone thought he'd be susceptible to bribery, but he's only got five hundred dollars of debt he needs to worry about right now. The rest—the student loans—he doesn't need to start paying them back until he graduates in two more years. That's a long time from the perspective of a college kid, and I don't think most of them worry that far into the future."

He set the files in his arm down on the table. "Read these too. I want you to look for clues in the files. Clues in the files only. You are not to leave the files unattended, and you are not to attempt any work outside this office."

"Is this what the chief had in mind when he said he wanted me in on the case? It was my understanding—"

His lips thinned. "The only thing you need to understand is that you do as I tell you. Yes, Chief Dobbins wants you on the case but, in the end, it's my case and if I tell him it's not working out, he'll agree to let you go."

I was about to give him a piece of my mind when Kate walked in. "Hey, Isabella! Great to see you here. Let's get lunch. I want to . . ."

She stopped speaking as she observed our faces. She turned around and left without saying another word.

"And there will be no friendly lunches with Kate. Is that understood?"

I couldn't take this sitting down, so I stood and stared him right in the eyes. "Detective Palmer, I hardly think you can tell me who I can and can't have lunch with."

"No, but I can keep Kate so busy she won't have time for you. Find me suspects I can investigate. That's your job. Look for signs of magic, but don't limit yourself to witch perps only."

I looked at the dozen thick files he'd left on the table. It would take me all day to read through them, checking details between files and making notes on suspects. I needed a notebook and a pot of coffee.

Out in the open office, I could hear Palmer talking to Kate. "Let her research and we'll take care of the police work."

I wasn't sure what to do about this. I decided to do nothing and see if anything changed over the course of the day. Once the chief saw me wasting my day reading files, he'd step in and I could tell Palmer I had nothing to do with it. I poured myself a cup of coffee I was sure had been on the burner overnight, added more creamer and sugar than was good for me, and grabbed a blank notebook from the supply cabinet.

The coffee was as bitter as I expected, but I still took sips of it. I wasn't sure if it was the caffeine or the flavor that kept me awake through the files, but it didn't matter. By lunchtime, I'd read all but four of the files assigned to me. I stood and stretched, rolling my stiff neck and shrugging my shoulders.

The office was almost empty, so I didn't need to worry about any accidental lunch invitations that Palmer could object to. I brought the files to Sergeant Wohan and asked him to keep an eye on them for me.

"You could have left them in the conference room," he said.

I shook my head. "Detective Palmer told me not to leave them unattended. Can I get you anything at the 7-Eleven?"

"No thanks. The wife packed my lunch for me."

I picked up a sandwich, a soda, and a large piece of chocolate cake at the store and brought it all back to the conference room, grabbing my files from Wohan on my way back. I ate lunch at the other end of the conference room table to keep the files clean. I woke up so early that it could be one of those days where my soda explodes all over the room because I wasn't paying attention to how much it got shaken up on the walk.

I was just starting my cake when the chief walked by. He did a double take when he saw me sitting alone. "You're not with Palmer?"

I shook my head and hastily swallowed the cake in my mouth. "No. He assigned me these files to read." I stood and handed him my notes. I'd only written a half page of notes all morning. "I wasn't able to find much that pointed to magic being used in the fire or the murder, and most of these files had nothing to do with the case."

He picked up a few and flipped through them. "No, they don't. I expected you would be out with Palmer, not here doing busywork."

I shrugged. "He made it clear that I was to do what he said, or he'd have me booted off the case entirely."

He rubbed his eyes. "I'll have a talk with him. We need you out in the field." He pulled out a chair and sat. "I hate to pry into your personal life, but do you see any chance of the two of you getting back together? That would make all this a lot easier."

"I don't think so. He saw me having dinner with another man last night and he was furious. He didn't do or say anything out of line, but as my date explained it, it was the microexpressions that gave him away."

The chief smiled. "If he's angry you're having dinner with another man, there's hope yet." He leaned forward, concern in his eyes. "Who was this guy? Do you want me to run a background check on him for you?"

"I don't think that's necessary. He's Christina's grandson." When the chief didn't seem to recognize who Christina was, I explained. "She's one of the members of the sorority. He works for the forestry department, keeping the trees in the state parks healthy and safe."

The chief looked perplexed. "You're dating a lumberjack?"

"Sort of, I guess. It was a short date and we didn't talk much about his work."

"Is he a witch, too?"

I nodded, impressed by how comfortable the chief was becoming with magic. "I get the feeling he doesn't use his powers very often though. Not all of us do. It's a lot easier to blend in that way."

"I suppose that's true. Anyway, I'll have a talk with Palmer, and we'll sort this out by the end of the day."

That was good to hear. I could finish today's files, but if I had to do this on a regular basis, I'd quit. Maybe that was what he wanted. Or maybe he wanted to keep me where he could see me so he'd know I was safe. "Thanks. I'll finish up these few files though. I don't want him thinking I'm not up to any job he gives me."

The chief left and I finished my cake before I got back to reading. Portsmouth was such a quiet town that even the people who had records didn't have exciting lives. I finished the last file and looked over my notes. I'd seen some telltale signs of petty magic in a few of them, but nothing that led to Bethany or the fire at the Fancy Tart.

I tidied up the files and put them all back on Palmer's desk, along with my notes. I had nothing else to do with my time and, since I'd gotten there so early, I decided to leave for the day. Palmer and I could talk in the morning. That didn't work out, because Palmer was coming in as I was leaving.

"We need to talk," he said.

"You know I've already worked a full day, going through those files. And let me tell you, most of them had nothing to do with this case. Were you trying to keep me sidelined? And what's your plan for tomorrow? More files? I doubt the chief is going to like that."

He glared at me. "In the conference room."

Once he closed the conference room door, I turned toward him and crossed my arms. I was ready to fight for a better place in the investigation, knowing I had the chief to back me up.

He sat and gestured for me to do the same. I remained standing.

"You don't make it easy, you know."

I raised an eyebrow.

"You take too many risks. I can accept you as an investigator, and even one with more resources than I'll ever have, but the way you throw yourself at danger like you're invincible—I can't take it. And that's why we are setting some very serious ground rules today. You need to agree to all of them to continue working on the case."

I wanted to ask him what would happen if I didn't, but we were talking and I'd worry about the consequences later. "What are the rules?"

"First of all, you will not investigate without a senior officer with you. That means me or the chief. I don't want you dragging Kate or Papatonis off on some ill-conceived chase. Their lives are also my responsibility, and it's one I take very seriously."

I nodded. I'd never put them in danger in the past, and I wouldn't in the future. "Okay. I can do that."

"Good. Second, you won't discuss the case with anyone. Not friends, not family, not even your cat."

I frowned. Not even Jameson? He knew what a valuable asset Jameson was. Why would he take away one of my greatest resources? "I agree with family and friends, but not Jameson. He knows too much to ignore his advice."

"No Jameson. I can't explain how a cat led me to solve a murder, and I can't make things up in my reports to hide his involvement."

What had he done on our previous cases? "Why not call him a confidential informant? Someone who insists on staying way off the books?"

He scowled. "CIs don't stay confidential for long. It might take longer for someone to figure out who he is, but eventually they will, and I'm not explaining to a judge how my information came from a talking cat. Every case I ever solved would come under scrutiny, and I'm not risking that."

Even though I was angry with him and didn't want to see any of his good points, I couldn't believe his cases wouldn't withstand scrutiny. "But you don't put anyone away who isn't guilty, do you?"

"I follow the clues. It's the judge and jury who decide what to do with a person. But no, I don't think anyone I've sent to jail is innocent. It's the guilty people who can fake innocence that I don't want to get out."

That made more sense. "Can I see the scene today? I need some sunlight and fresh air."

Chapter 6

We took his car to what was left of the Fancy Tart. Businesses on both sides of the bakery were open, but had a somber air. Employees were dressed in black, and there were signs in their windows telling everyone about the charitable donations they were collecting for the bakery's employees who were suddenly out of work.

The bakery was completely destroyed. The glass windows were shattered and covered by plywood. I knew the inside would look worse.

Palmer unlocked the door and handed me a flashlight. "Power's out, so you'll need this."

I turned it on and followed him inside. The smell hit me first. Burned bread, yeast that had started to grow unchecked, and melted plastic. I swung the light around the dining area. Tables and chairs had been pushed up against the walls to make room for the firefighters. The counter at the back was scorched and pastries inside it were soggy and burned.

A half-melted sign with the day's specials hung precariously from the wall. I choked back a sob as I recognized Bethany's handwriting.

"Feel anything magical?" Palmer asked.

I shook my head. "I need Jameson, or at least Thea and Delia here to help me with that."

He turned to look at me. "You do? I didn't think there were many limits on your abilities."

I looked at the melted point-of-sale system. Bethany hadn't wanted to spend money on it, saying an old-fashioned register would work fine, but her brother had talked her into it. After all the difficulties she had setting it up, she might be smiling down on us, happy it was ruined.

Palmer led me to the kitchen, where the smell intensified.

"Can we open a window?"

He looked around, but they were all boarded over. "I'll open the back door, but that's the best we can do."

I swept my flashlight around the room, looking for the origin of the fire. All four walls were equally burned, and the linoleum on the floor had melted and buckled everywhere. Yellow evidence markers dotted the room, and several were concentrated by the door to Bethany's office. An outline had been taped on the floor.

Fresh air and light entered the kitchen as Palmer opened the back door.

"Is this . . ." I asked, pointing to her office door.

"Yes. She was found here. There was blood in her office as well. We think she tried to escape the fire, but died before she could. The ME is still working on a timeline for us."

I looked up at him, tears in my eyes. I wanted to rest my head on his shoulder and have him tell me we'd figure everything out. I knew we would, but I wanted a little reassurance.

He stood with his arms crossed. "Do you need to see anything else?"

I looked into her office. "The safe is empty. Was it like that yesterday?"

"Yes. It was opened and emptied before the fire started."

Maybe this was a robbery gone bad. "Any fingerprints? Any clues at all?"

"No prints we can use. I want your take on the scene before we go over the clues."

I took a quick walk through the rest of the kitchen, but didn't see anything that led me to believe magic had been used there. "I'm done. It doesn't look like magic had been used here but, if you want me to be certain, I need to call someone else in."

"Fine. Call Jameson in."

Hey, Jameson. Can you come to the Fancy Tart? I need a quick check on whether magic was used here.

Without a word, he appeared at my feet. Palmer and I watched as he walked through the kitchen, into Bethany's office, and finally into the dining area. *No magic here.*

"He says no magic was used here. So I guess you don't need me on the case."

"You're right. I don't. But if you promise to behave yourself, you can stay."

I hadn't expected that. I thought for sure he'd want me gone as soon as possible. But then again, the chief had already told him to bring me onto the case, and maybe he couldn't get rid of me. Would I continue to follow Palmer's rules? I wasn't so sure. "Thanks. I want to find out who did this to my friend."

He locked the back door and we left, Jameson trotting behind us. I turned my face up to the weak spring sun and let go of the pain I felt walking through my friend's murder scene. I needed to focus on finding her killer. "What've we got for clues?"

Palmer looked to Jameson. "Thanks for your help."

Jameson, who never took a hint he didn't want to, walked away. He probably had more important things to do, like devise new and creative ways to make my training as difficult as possible.

"Let me drive you home," Palmer said. "We'll talk clues on the way."

I could easily have walked home myself but, if he wanted to be nice to me, I wasn't going to stop him.

He started the car and pulled out into traffic. "I can't make up my mind whether the murder was planned or not. Every aspect of it seems unrehearsed and, yet, there aren't any solid clues to work with."

"Do you think her killer just got lucky and the fire destroyed anything he might have left behind?" I asked.

"Could be. We've got the knife, and it looks like the one missing from the kitchen. Anyone could have picked it up."

I looked out the window at the familiar street. "Not anyone. It was an early morning fire, so she'd have let her killer in." I blew out a breath because, as I thought about it, that didn't narrow the list of suspects down as much as I'd hoped. "Delivery drivers, employees, someone coming in for an interview, surprise health inspections—there are a lot of people to look at."

We pulled into my parking lot. "I'm interviewing her brother tomorrow. He might shed some light on who would want to see her dead, and what was in the safe. I'd like you there."

I nodded. "What time?"

"I'll pick you up at eight, then we'll go get him."

Just like old times, except two months ago he'd have smiled at me instead of the almost perpetual scowl he had now.

Bruce opened his door as I walked by. I held up my hand to stop him from speaking. "Not today."

Once in my apartment, I went straight to the bathroom and started running a bath. I needed to put my thoughts in order. I chose rose-scented bubble bath and waited for the water to warm up. As I climbed into the tub, I let my grief spill out. Once I was done crying, I washed the tears from my face and started to think. Who would have motive to kill Bethany?

She and her brother had not always gotten along well since I'd known them. He wanted to modernize the business and she resisted. They argued, but did they get angry enough for murder? I wasn't sure about that.

As much as I didn't like the idea, Omar needed some thought. What if he went in to quit early in the morning and they fought? He had always seemed gentle and kind to me, but people could get weird about money, and anger could make people do things they'd regret.

At six I called my mother to see how the day went.

"Just fine. No issues at all," she said.

"Thanks, mom. I really appreciate you stepping in for me. Can you do it again tomorrow? Palmer and I are going to start interviewing suspects."

"Of course I can. Why don't I plan to be at the shop until you tell me otherwise? It's a nice change of pace, and I like talking to the customers."

I poured myself a glass of water. "That would be great."

"In fact, I was thinking about applying for the opening you have."

So much for the sense of relief I felt. I love my mother, but working together on a permanent basis sounded like something out of my worst nightmares. And if I ever thought I needed to fire her? I shuddered. No. I could not hire my mother. "Maybe we'll talk about that later. I need to concentrate on the case first."

Once we hung up, I went straight to my laptop to read résumés of people who had applied for my opening. If I could hire someone quickly, I could avoid telling her I didn't want to work with her.

Chapter 7

I finished reading résumés by seven thirty and was starving. A quick look in my refrigerator told me I needed to set aside some time for grocery shopping and cooking. Tonight I'd have to head over to Proctor House and see what Aunt Nadia had in the fridge.

I opened the kitchen door of Proctor House to the scent of burgers and fries. The table had small plates of everything a person could want on their burger—three types of cheese, bacon, lettuce, tomato, raw onion, sauteed onion, pickles, and then bottles of condiments at the end of the table.

Aunt Nadia was scooping fries out of hot oil. "Hi, sweetie. I hope you're hungry. I may have made too many sliders."

I hung up my coat. "No such thing."

The rest of the family arrived and we started serving ourselves. I was on my second bite of bacon and bleu cheese burger when Grandma decided to drop a bombshell.

"I've decided to sell the house."

Everyone else at the table stared at her, mouths agape. Delia was the first to regain her composure. "What do you mean, sell the house?"

Grandma was ready for the confrontation. "It's not a difficult sentence, Delia. Sell the house, divide the money, and go live somewhere warmer and calmer. I'm not getting any younger, and there's a beautiful island in the Caribbean only open to witches. I'd like to live there and give my joints a rest from the winter cold."

I couldn't believe what I was hearing. Our family had owned this house since before Portsmouth was even a town. "How long have you been thinking about this?"

"Hope first brought the idea up. She's exhausted by running the sorority and wants to retire. I don't blame her and her descriptions of retirement, quite honestly, sound like fun. And fun isn't something I've had in a long while here."

Delia set her slider down. "But why so far away?"

Grandma, who was sitting between Thea and Delia, took Delia's hand. "We'll make sure the three of you can teleport before I go, and then it's not far at all." She smiled at a thought. "In fact, you could commute from the island to Portsmouth every day if you wanted to."

I didn't like that idea at all. It would be a lot harder to connect with my customers if I went home to a tropical island every night. "Do you need to sell the house?"

My mother looked uneasy. "We were thinking of going with her. We're not that old, but white sand and a warm ocean sounds perfect to me."

Thea pointed a pickle spear at my mother. "When you say we, do you mean all three aunts?"

Aunt Lily nodded. "We had planned to tell you soon." She shot a scowl at Grandma. "But maybe not so abruptly."

"The house would be too big for you three. It would be difficult for you to keep up with the wards," my mother said.

Where had this thought come from? Grandma loved Proctor House, and I thought she'd never leave Portsmouth. "No. I'm sorry. I don't like this at all. You're taking away our home and the safest house in the city, all so you can sit on a beach and drink mai tais? I vote no, you can't sell the house."

"I'm with Isabella," Thea said.

Delia nodded. "Me too. We don't want anyone to move, but we can't stop you from that. But at least don't sell the house. You know eventually we'll have kids and we're going to need a house to raise them in. And the three of us will want to live together."

I poured myself a glass of water. This all seemed so hasty and unplanned. Grandma made snap decisions often, but they were usually better choices than this. "When were you planning to move? You're not leaving us with the fraternity on the loose, are you? If nothing else, the sorority needs Hope to keep us together."

My mother tried to soothe us. "We hadn't picked a date yet. There's a lot to do before we could leave, including making sure you girls have everything you need, magically speaking. There's still a lot of training we can give you."

"And don't forget, you each have a familiar. You won't be alone. And we can come to you at a moment's notice," Aunt Nadia said.

"I still want the house," I said. "I'd be willing to give up my apartment for it."

All eyes turned to me. Apparently, no one thought I'd ever come back. "What? The house is important, and I can't imagine Proctor House having anyone but Proctors living in it." I'd always imagined Thea, Delia, and me raising our children in the house, just as the aunts had. Grandma's sisters had moved out, away from the protection of the house, and they'd died years ago.

"Girls, it isn't that big of a deal. I suppose we don't have to sell the house. We can always pop in to help you with the wards until you get the hang of them," Aunt Lily said.

"Dinner is getting cold," Aunt Nadia said. "Why don't we finish eating, and we'll plan to discuss this again later, closer to when we're planning to go."

Did they already have a timeline? This sounded more planned out than they were admitting to. "And when is that?" I asked.

My mother sighed. "Not for a while still. Eat and we'll talk more later. I promise."

We spent the rest of dinner not talking to each other. The aunts didn't want to set off another round of questions, and Thea, Delia, and I were each thinking about what this move would mean for us.

I opened my apartment door to find Jameson waiting for me. "Did you know about this?"

He tilted his head. "Know about what?"

Acting innocent was a sure sign of guilt for my familiar. "About the aunts and Grandma moving to some island in the Caribbean. When did you know they were planning this?"

"They've been talking about it for a while now, but they swore us to secrecy."

How could that be? "I thought you were my familiar. Shouldn't you be looking out for me instead of keeping someone else's secrets?" The more I thought about it, the angrier I got. "Maybe you should explain exactly where your loyalties lie, because if I can't trust you to tell me what I need to know, I'm not sure you're the right familiar for me."

I closed my mouth. I'd already said more in anger than I'd wanted to. I wasn't sure how far I could go with our witch–familiar relationship, because I'd never had reason to question it before. Could he leave me and, if he did, would he take the amulet and my membership in the Sorority of Brigid with him? "Never mind. Don't answer those questions. I'm going to bed."

It took effort, but I didn't slam my bedroom door. I felt like my whole life was turned on its end—no Palmer, no Grandma, no aunts, and no Proctor House. How could we—Thea, Delia, and I—live without the rest of the family? Surely we'd need at least one of the aunts to stay with us, like Grandma had done for her daughter and nieces.

I kicked off my boots and lay on the bed. Was the goddess testing us?

Twenty minutes later, there was a knock at the apartment door. Delia and Thea waved at me when I looked through the peephole. I was crabby and didn't want to talk to anyone. Even Jameson was leaving me alone for now. But I opened the door and let them in anyway.

"I don't want to talk about it," I said.

Delia smiled at me. "Too bad, because we've got a plan."

I arched an eyebrow, inviting her to tell me more.

Thea and Delia sat on the couch and I joined them, perching on the arm.

Delia started to explain. "There's nothing we can do to keep Grandma and the aunts in Portsmouth. And do we want to keep them here if they want to move? No."

Thea chimed in. "All we need to do is buy the house. We can't afford all of it but, if you pitch in, and they sell it to us at a slight discount, we can manage."

"How much is the house worth?" I asked.

Thea blew out a breath. "It's the largest lot within miles, and in this economy its price is inflated. That's why we need them to give us a discount. We were thinking, between the three of us, we could swing one million for it."

My eyes bulged at the price. "I couldn't afford my share of that. How much are you charging these days for tours?"

"We've been saving. Free room and board lets us put almost everything we make into the bank," Delia said.

"Let's think for a minute here. Did Grandma buy the house from anyone, or did she just assume ownership by continuing to live there? And can't we do the same thing?" I asked.

Thea shrugged. "Not sure about that."

I was confused. "But Aunt Lily said they wouldn't need to sell it, they could just give it to us. So why buy it?"

Delia ran her hand through her hair. "This is their retirement, Isabella. I don't want them to scrimp and save every penny for necessities. This is the only way we could give them money that they'd accept."

She was right. If they were determined to leave, I didn't want to stop them, or take away the money they'd have by selling the house.

But Proctor House needed to be owned by Proctor witches. I was sure of that.

Chapter 8

I tossed and turned all that night, not wanting to think about my future, but still obsessing over it. I went so far as to consider moving to an island with the family. If we all went, that island might not know what hit it.

My alarm went off at seven, and I dragged my tired body into the shower. Usually I was awake and ready to go by the time I was done, but I needed twenty seconds of ice cold water to jump-start my brain and make sure I didn't climb back into bed. My new working relationship with Palmer had me feeling like I needed to prove myself to him all over again.

I had to demonstrate how responsible, careful, and prudent I was. It was a lot of work on my part, just to make sure I'd be around when he needed me.

Jameson was waiting for me in the kitchen. "Double training tonight since I let you have last night off."

I squinted at him. "Let me have the night off? I wouldn't have been any good last night and, honestly, I won't be any good tonight either." I leaned up against the counter, fighting to keep myself from crying. "Have some compassion, my friend is dead, and I need to spend what energy I have working with Palmer to find her killer."

He didn't say anything else, and I wasn't sure that he knew what compassion even was. I made myself coffee and dressed in my most professional outfit. Black pants and a white button-down shirt. I threw a sweater on over the shirt and was ready to go. I wasn't sure what he had planned for me today other than our meeting with Andrew. I hoped I'd passed whatever test reading all those files had to be and I'd never have to do that again.

I stood outside in the bitter wind, waiting for him to arrive. I used a warming spell on my hands, toes, and ears to take the edge off the wind.

Palmer pulled up. "Ready to go?"

As if I would be standing out here if I wasn't. Remain pleasant, I reminded myself, don't get kicked off the case.

I started walking toward Palmer's car, ice-cold wind whipping my hair around my face. Teleportation would make my life so much easier, but I couldn't get a handle on how to do it properly. It was frustrating, because most things came much more easily to me.

I reached for the handle. "Only if you don't force me to read files all day again today."

I wasn't sure how that was a viable negotiation tactic, but he gave me a small smile.

"If you insist. Get in before you freeze."

I climbed in and he handed me a travel mug. "Irish breakfast tea. There's a blueberry muffin in the paper bag too."

What was going on here? Why was he being so nice to me? There was a second travel mug in the center console, so he'd made one specifically for me. I pulled a still-warm muffin out of the bag. "Thanks. Homemade?"

He nodded.

So he was stress baking again. Because he was back to working with me? "Did you get any sleep last night or were you up worrying?"

He didn't answer my question. "Quick change of plan. We're going to pick up Omar and interrogate him this morning. Is that something you can do, or should you watch instead? I don't want your friendship with him getting in the way of the investigation."

I took a sip of tea and thought for a moment. "Are you forgetting how comfortable people are telling me things? Maybe I should interrogate him and you should stay behind the mirror."

Palmer frowned. "How about we play that by ear. We'll start together."

I nodded and started nibbling on my muffin. What possible reason would Omar have to kill Bethany? I hadn't worked at the Fancy Tart for over a year now, but every time I was there for coffee and pastries they seemed to work well together. "Do you really think Omar did it? Killed her and then set the building on fire? It doesn't seem like him."

Palmer stopped at a red light and looked at me. "It doesn't. On the other hand, we've both seen some unbelievable things during our investigations, so we're not ruling anyone out."

"That's fair. I hope you've got a long list of people to talk to though."

We didn't say anything else for the rest of the ride to Omar's apartment. I wanted to talk about us, but I couldn't come up with a gentle way to start the conversation. I decided we should wait until after we'd spent more time together.

We pulled up in front of Omar's apartment building. "Is he expecting us?"

Palmer nodded.

I pursed my lips. "Is this a test? If he's here and waiting, he's probably innocent?"

"It is. Had someone watching the place all night and he didn't go anywhere. If he tried to leave town, Papatonis would have followed him."

I wondered if he'd done the same thing to me when I'd first met him and he was convinced I'd killed my mentor, Trina. He probably did, but I wasn't going to ask him. I didn't need to know.

We got out of the car and rang Omar's doorbell. A crackly voice told us he'd be right down.

When Omar opened the door, his eyes widened to see me, then he smiled. "Good morning. Ready to get this over with?"

Once the three of us were settled into an interrogation room, Palmer started to talk. "Look, Omar, I don't know you all that well, but you've waited on me more than enough times that I feel like we've got a good rapport going on. Would you agree?"

Omar nodded.

"Then the first thing I'm going to ask you is are you sure you don't want an attorney with you? We can provide one for you, or you can call one of your own."

Omar sat back in his chair, looking more relaxed than he should be. "Nah. I don't need an attorney, because I didn't set fire to the building and I certainly didn't kill Bethany."

"Think about this," I urged him. "Police are trained to make you trip up and find holes in your story. And lawyers are trained to keep you from making those mistakes."

He didn't change his pose. "I'd like to get out of here as quickly as possible, because I've got to find a new job. Rent doesn't pay itself."

Palmer shook his head as if to say he tried to warn him. "We've had reports that you'd been arguing with Bethany. What was that about?"

"The number of hours she made me work. I've been taking on more hours and more responsibilities, and I haven't seen a raise or any other benefits either. First Isabella left and Abby and I split her hours and workload, then Abby left and Bethany didn't hire anyone to replace either of them. She expected me to work a full week, then be available for emergencies on my time off. I told her I couldn't keep it up, and she needed to hire another person, if not two. My grades were starting to slip, and I couldn't have that."

"So you were angry at how she was treating you?"

Omar nodded, and I realized Palmer wasn't even recording. I couldn't believe Bethany hadn't hired anyone else. "But the overtime pay must have been nice," I said.

Omar laughed. "No overtime. She said she couldn't afford it and that I'd have no job if she had to pay me so much." He sat up and leaned his elbows on the table. "I decided a job was better than none, but that I'd start looking for another one right away."

"Any luck?" I asked.

He shook his head. "Nothing good."

He could replace Mackenzie. That would be great for me, because I already knew we got along and could work well together. I bit my lip to keep from offering him the job during the interrogation. Palmer would see that as another impulsive, dangerous act.

"All this is great, but the question comes down to your alibi. Where were you two nights ago?" Palmer asked.

"I left work after we argued and went back to my apartment. I paced around the living room for about ten minutes and then went out for a run."

"Where did you go?"

"I did ten loops around Prescott Park. The bank across the street has a camera and you'll be able to see me."

Palmer frowned. "Ten loops, what's that? Eight miles?"

"Six. I was there for an hour, then I went back to my apartment. I took a shower then spent a few hours on the roof terrace drinking with my neighbor, talking about what lousy lives we had."

Palmer pulled his notebook out and started writing. "Your neighbor's name?"

"Julianna Cabot."

"What did you do after that?" Palmer asked.

"I spent the night at her place. I woke up the next morning to Isabella's call."

Palmer stood up. "We'll have to check your alibi."

Was that it? Were we done? I definitely had the feeling Omar wasn't our murderer, but I was surprised Palmer had come to the same conclusion so quickly.

Omar nodded. "Not a problem."

We scrambled to get up and follow Palmer as he left the interrogation room. Palmer tossed me his keys. "Drive him home, would you? Then we'll go see the brother."

I reached out and grabbed the keys from the air, grateful I didn't miss them. "Sure thing." I was astonished he was letting me drive his car. He was acting like an entirely different man today—bringing me breakfast and trusting me with his car.

"I can't believe she treated you so badly," I said as I unlocked Palmer's car.

Omar sat and shook his head. "I don't know what was going on, but she was having a tough time of it after you left."

I started the car and reversed out of the parking spot. "It was always so busy. She must have been making a profit."

"She might have been, but I got the feeling she wasn't getting along with Andrew. Once you and Abby left, there was more tension in the bakery. Neither of them said anything to me, but they'd stop talking when I went out back."

I looked at him quickly. "Maybe they were talking about you?"

"I don't think that was it, because there was tension between them, but none between either of them and me, at least not until I started to complain about my working conditions."

I stopped the car in front of his building. "I was thinking, once this is all over, would you like to come work for me?"

He grinned. "What? Really? I'd love to. When can I start?"

"Let's wait until you're officially cleared. Detective Palmer would have a fit if I hired a suspect in one of his investigations."

"He tells you how to run your business?" Omar asked.

I shook my head. "No. But he broke up with me because he said I did too many dangerous things, so I'm trying to be better."

Omar raised an eyebrow.

"No, I'm not letting him tell me what to do. But he's right. I don't always think before I act, and I'm lucky I haven't been hurt yet." At least not hurt much.

"If you say so. Thanks for the ride."

As he got out of the car, I told him I'd call once he could start at the apothecary. I drove off, relieved to have found a suitable replacement for Mackenzie.

Chapter 9

I drove back to the station, wondering what Bethany and Andrew had been fighting about. Palmer was waiting outside for me and I felt sorry for him—he had no warmth spell.

I got out of the car so he could drive. "I offered Omar a job at the apothecary once you clear him."

He pulled out into traffic and had nothing to say. After what seemed like an hour of driving, even though the clock said it had been three minutes, Palmer smiled. "That was nice of you."

What was with the smile and the compliment? I was just getting used to the Palmer who was all business and had no time for me unless I was working for him. Hiring Omar might have been nice, but it was also good for me. "I suppose so, but hiring Omar is a lot easier than reading through résumés and interviewing people. At least I know him and know he's going to do what I ask him." I shifted in my seat to look at him. "What's the plan for the rest of the day?"

"We're going to talk to her brother and see where that takes us. You've worked with him, so I want you to pay particular attention to how he reacts to my questions."

I nodded. "Okay, but I can't imagine he would kill his own sister."

Palmer turned left on Islington Street. "You and your cousins seem to get along well, but trust me, siblings can have the fiercest hate."

That was sad. If there was one thing in this world I knew I could count on, it was Thea and Delia, who were as close as sisters to me. I couldn't imagine what life would be like if I couldn't rely on them. And I was sure they felt the same. "I can't imagine."

I faced front again because I couldn't look at him as I asked the next question. "So . . . are we talking again?"

He sighed. "It's not like that. It was never like that. I just can't—my heart can't take watching you throw yourself into danger. I've never dated anyone like you—"

I snorted. "I bet you haven't. Or if you have ever dated a witch before, she didn't tell you her secret."

He looked at me quickly. "Probably not, but I mean I've never dated someone who had a dangerous life. I'm not used to worrying about the people I love like that."

I didn't respond to that bombshell. Palmer loved me? As in currently, at this moment, he loved me? My heart began to race, because I was pretty sure I loved him too. This was the best news, and the worst news all at once.

I couldn't give up my work with the sorority and, even if I did, I wasn't sure the fraternity would leave me alone, so I had to keep throwing myself at danger. I sighed. Our relationship was never going to work out. "You don't worry about everyone else you work with?"

He bit his lip. "That's different. We expect it. My marriage might have been horrible in a lot of ways, but I knew my wife was never in danger on a daily basis. It was comforting, and I don't have that with you."

"True, you don't. But I hope we had a better relationship overall when"—my breath caught—"when we were together."

He pulled into the driveway of a white house and shut the car off. "Don't get out yet. We need to finish this conversation."

I nodded but still didn't look at him. I couldn't face another rejection right now.

He reached over and took my hand in his. "I was angry that day outside Proctor House, and I said some things that maybe I shouldn't have.

Or at least I should have waited to cool down. The moment I saw how much I upset you, I felt horrible. I should have waited until I was calmer before I said anything. I'm sorry."

I willed myself not to cry. He'd hurt me badly that day, and I never thought I'd hear an apology from him. "But you still feel the same, so we might as well go talk to Andrew."

"I don't know that I do. It was easy to hold to our break up when I didn't see you, but yesterday was difficult. You were just one office away and I wanted to go in and talk, grab lunch with you, and go back to the way we were. But I couldn't have that conversation in the office."

He frowned. "And when I saw you on that date, I was so angry. I hated seeing you with a guy your own age, having fun, and I thought you couldn't feel the same for me, not if you were so quick to replace me."

I couldn't take it anymore. I brushed a tear off my cheek and turned to him. "My date? That was Christina's grandson, and my mother forced me to go out with him. Well, okay, she didn't force me, but she said if I went out with him once, she'd stop trying to set me up."

Palmer furrowed his eyebrows. "I got a coupon for free food at the same restaurant but it expired that day. If I'd known you were there, I'd have gone somewhere else."

A woman in jeans and a sweater left the house and knocked on Palmer's window. "Can I help you?"

Palmer flashed his badge and rolled down his window. "Police business, ma'am. We're surveilling the neighborhood. We'll be out of your way in another ten minutes."

Her eyes widened. "Is everything okay? I mean, I have kids. Should I keep them inside today?"

He flashed her his most reassuring smile. "No ma'am. This is just routine policework. You and your family are safe here in the neighborhood."

She walked away and he rolled his window up. I started to giggle. "Official police business? Since when does this qualify as work time?"

"Since you're all I can think about and I need your help. You know the suspects and are the best person to close the case with me."

I was all he could think about? Really? "Okay, so where do we go from here? I'm not ready to say all is forgotten."

He squeezed my hand. "Do you think we can work together? As colleagues?"

I nodded. "I think so." I debated telling him I'd agreed to go out with Liam again, but it wasn't any of his business right now.

He pulled the car out of the driveway and continued down the street.

"I can't believe you pulled into a random driveway just to talk," I said.

He grinned. "The house looked empty. I've been waiting for the right time to apologize to you, and I couldn't do it while we were driving. You deserve better than that."

My heart fluttered, and I found I wasn't so excited for my second date with Liam. As much as I liked being with someone who understood life as a witch, he was a bit . . . dull compared to Palmer.

"Since neither of us think Andrew killed Bethany, we're going in looking like a condolence and sympathy call. I want you to take the lead, with sympathy, and we'll both watch him."

I could do that. "I know I said I didn't think he could have killed her, but I've seen them fighting about the bakery. He wanted to have a share in the business, and she wanted to keep him as an employee. He thought because he was family that he deserved to be a partner."

He rolled his eyes. "You have no idea how lucky you are to have your family. Has anyone tried to take a part of the apothecary from you?"

Of course they hadn't. And they wouldn't, even if they did work there. "No. It's not theirs, it's mine. I'm not sure where Andrew's sense of entitlement comes from."

"If we play our cards right, he'll tell us."

We made a good interrogation team, so I was sure he would. Palmer pulled into another driveway. This time, the house was a small, red, one-story building that needed a new roof. "Is this the house, or do we need to talk more?" I asked.

Palmer chuckled. "This is the house. I wonder if he wanted a share of the business because Bethany wasn't paying him well."

I shrugged. I had no idea what he made, but I couldn't see Bethany keeping him at minimum wage, not with all the years he'd worked for her. "I don't know. You'll have to look at the bank records to figure that out."

He turned to look at me. "We're good for now? You don't hate me?"

My heart sank. I never hated him, I was only confused and hurt by his actions. "Of course not. You'd have to work really hard to get me to hate you. I'm fine working with you on this case, but nothing more."

Was it my imagination, or did his shoulders slump? Was he hoping for more? He needed to earn back my trust before I was willing to return to our personal relationship.

Chapter 10

Whoever said you couldn't judge a book by its cover had never compared the inside and outside of Andrew's house. I peered through the front door window before I rang the doorbell. The house looked like he hated closets and any sort of storage container. Clothing was everywhere, along with random objects covering every surface of the kitchen and living room. Pens, dirty mugs, newspapers, a half-buried laptop, and several broken lamps were strewn about.

I pressed the doorbell, but there was no sound. Palmer reached past me and banged on the door. After a moment we heard indistinct grumbling, then saw a disheveled Andrew making his way through the living room to us.

As he opened the door, his frowned deepened. "Can't a man grieve in peace?"

I tried not to look horrified. He looked terrible and smelled worse. His red, puffy eyes were set off by the dark circles under them. He smelled like stale beer and massive deodorant failure. I had planned to give him a hug, but couldn't bring myself to move closer to him. "Hi, Andrew. I wanted to stop by and say how sorry I was about Bethany."

He coughed and then wiped his nose on the arm of his shirt. "Sorry. I've got a cold. Did you have to bring the police with you?"

I gave him a small smile. "You remember Detective Palmer. He's my ride, and when I said I wanted to talk to you, he offered to come along." I braced myself for the next question.

"Can we come in?" I didn't want to go into his house, but we wouldn't get very far talking on his front stairs.

Andrew opened the door for us. "If you can stand the mess, sure."

Palmer and I walked in, and I looked around for a spot to sit. No luck. Palmer stood behind me, very close, as though he was making sure he could protect me. I didn't need to be protected from Andrew, but if there was anything living under the piles of clothing and junk, I'd be happy to let Palmer take care of it.

"Can I get you something to drink? I'm sure I can find a clean glass around here somewhere," Andrew said.

I shook my head. "Oh no, that's not necessary. We'll only be here for a few minutes."

Andrew didn't look any better than his house, but that was to be expected. "How are you holding up?" I asked.

Andrew shrugged. "I don't know. I can't believe she's gone, you know?"

I nodded. "It's a shock. She was so kind to me."

He frowned. "Yeah, she was nice to a lot of people."

Palmer put his hand on my shoulder. "But not you?"

"You got any siblings?" Andrew asked. "We had the usual disagreements. And when your sister moves from being your bossy older sister to your actual boss, well, it's not easy."

After an uneasy time where no one spoke, I continued on with my thoughts on Bethany. "She was so helpful when I inherited the apothecary. I had no idea how to run a business, and she took all the time I needed to explain things like payroll, ordering supplies, and even how to deal with some very difficult customers. I'm not sure I'd have made it through this first year of business without her guidance."

I felt like a heel for having such fond memories when Andrew didn't, but I wanted him to talk more about her.

Andrew walked into the kitchen and took a beer out of his refrigerator. He held it up as though to ask if Palmer and I wanted one. I shook my head and Palmer said, "No thanks."

Andrew pushed a pile of socks off the arm of a couch and sat. "Your loss, then. It's better to get an early start on the day when you're unemployed. I've got to go out and find a new job and, with Bethany dead, I don't even have a reference. It's not going to be easy to find something before the next mortgage payment is due."

"I've worked with you. I'd be happy to give you a reference," I said. "And besides that, everyone in town has eaten at the Fancy Tart at least once. We all know how good a pastry chef you are. I'm sure it won't be long until you land on your feet again."

He opened his beer and drank half the can at once. He wasn't kidding about getting an early start.

"If you were so unhappy, why didn't you leave?" I asked.

He squinted at me. "Why do you think? If I left, I'd never have a claim on my share of the business. I'd have no job, and who knows what kind of lies she'd spread about me if she learned I wanted to leave."

I shook my head. This didn't seem like the Bethany I knew and loved. She was kind, and I thought since she always looked out for me, she looked out for everyone. Then again, siblings have their own dynamic.

Palmer cleared his throat. "It must be difficult knowing that if you'd been there you could have saved her."

Andrew took a swig of his beer and belched. "I would have been, but I can't shake this cold." He pushed a pile of clothing off the couch and sank down onto it.

Palmer frowned. "How long have you been sick?"

Andrew shrugged. "Four or five days. I went to urgent care and they told me to drink lots of fluids and rest."

I held in a shudder. I was pretty sure they didn't mean hydrate with beer.

"I've got some tea that would help you rest, if you think you'll have problems sleeping," I offered.

Andrew crushed the empty can and tossed it toward the table. It slid off and landed on top of a soiled apron from the Fancy Tart. "Everything I need is here. I don't need some fancy tea to help me rest. Anyway, I texted Bethany and she told me to take the day off."

I spared a thought for his liver before I continued. "I understand. If you change your mind, let me know, or just stop by the apothecary and we can take care of you."

"Can I see this message?" Palmer asked.

Andrew pointed to the kitchen. "It's in there somewhere."

I couldn't imagine touching anything in that kitchen, but I didn't have to. Palmer sacrificed himself and went in. He returned and held up a cell phone. The screen was cracked at each corner and the upper left corner was blank, cutting off the head of the beautiful woman on Andrew's screen. Palmer handed Andrew the phone. "This your phone? Can you show me the text message?"

Andrew squinted at Palmer. "Don't you need a warrant?"

Palmer nodded. "I can get one if you don't want to show me the text. I don't want to search the phone, just confirm your sister's text."

Andrew unlocked his phone and scrolled through his messages. He pulled up Bethany's and held it up for Palmer and me to confirm the message. Once we'd read it, he locked the phone and shoved it into his pants pocket. "Okay? I've got to call a funeral director and get everything set up."

Palmer wasn't done questioning him, though. "Do you have a copy of her will?"

Andrew shook his head. "No. But I'm sure she didn't leave anything to me, not even enough to bury her. Figures she'd take advantage of me right to the very end." He stood up. "I'm getting another beer. You two can see yourselves out."

Once we left his dingy house, I took a deep breath of fresh air. "Well, that was terrible. I don't even know how I can help him."

Palmer opened the car door for me. I looked up at him, confused. "Old habits, don't read anything into it."

It was too late for that. He never opened doors for Kate, not even on the one social event we'd all been on—the station's holiday party. I smiled. "Of course not. We're just coworkers."

"Let's talk about the files you read," he said.

I winced. "Please don't tell me you're giving me more to read. My soul may shrivel and die if I need to read any more dry, boring reports." Not to mention I was going to have nightmares about arson for weeks, until my subconscious fully worked through the horrors of what I'd read over the past two days.

"Did you see any patterns between older fires and the one at the Fancy Tart?"

I hadn't. But I did see some very concerning similarities between several fires set over the past decade. "Nothing that looked like the one at the Tart, but I saw some that looked the same that hadn't been cross-referenced. I made a note of the cases on the paper I put on top of the files. There are eight, maybe nine cases that look like they could be from the same person."

He frowned but said nothing.

I didn't understand why he looked upset. I might have found a common thread that could lead to solving several arsons. "Are you upset? Should I not have wasted my time there?"

"No, it's not that. It's that we should have caught it already. And if we didn't, the fire marshal should have." He sighed. "This is why I like having you on my team. You see things we miss."

My heart cracked, just a little bit. "I'm still available if you need me. We can set aside our personal issues and just work cases together." I wasn't sure how well I could do that, but the thought of getting justice for the people affected by those nine fires made me want to try.

"Maybe we can try, for important cases. But I've got to spend the rest of the day at my desk. Where can I drop you off?"

I thought for a minute. "My mother's running the apothecary for me today, but I can always spend more time in the prep room." Would I finally have a day to devote to new products?

"No problem."

We didn't talk for the rest of the drive, which suited me just fine. He seemed to be saying he wanted me near him in one sentence, but that he didn't think we should spend time together in the next. I wasn't sure what I wanted either. Last week I would have said I wanted to be with him but, after my date with Liam, I wasn't so sure. Liam was so relaxing to be around because we had the same background, had the same beliefs and moral compass. Maybe this was why people often chose partners from their own religion.

He pulled up to the front of the apothecary. "I'll call you tonight and let you know if there've been any developments. We can talk about our plan for tomorrow too."

That sounded good to me. "Okay. I've missed days of training, and I think Jameson wants me to make them all up tonight, so I won't be able to talk much."

Palmer shook his head. "I still have a hard time believing all this, you know."

I nodded. "Understandable. But you're doing better than we expected, and you should give yourself credit for that."

Chapter 11

I walked into the apothecary and heard laughing. My mother was laughing with a man. In my office. What was going on here? "Mom?"

She walked into the shop, face glowing with happiness, and behind her walked Alex. I still had no idea what was going on. She took my hand and said, "Have we got a surprise for you. Let's go sit in the office."

I followed them back to the office and sat behind my desk. Alex was grinning too. I wasn't sure I'd seen him smile more than once or twice. "Okay, what's up?" I asked.

My mother took a deep breath. She looked at Alex and took another one. When she still didn't speak, he took her hand. "Do you want me to tell her?"

Why was my security guard holding my mother's hand? They'd never met before today. Was there some sort of rogue love spell in the air?

"No, I'll do it," my mother said to him. "Isabella, I'd like you to meet your father."

I sat still, looking from one to the other. What kind of joke was this? My father had abandoned us when I was very young, and my mother said he would never be back. She never seemed angry at him, though. Just sad and resigned.

They looked at each other and grinned. Alex brought my mother's hand to his lips.

"Okay, what in the world is going on here? Mother, did you cast some sort of love spell on my security guard? Did someone spike your coffee with a love spell? You two haven't met before today."

Alex took a locket from his pocket. "It's true. I'm sorry I couldn't tell you. I didn't want you to know now, but Em said she didn't think she could keep the secret, not now that she knew I was in town."

Em? He'd once told me his wife's name was Em, but I thought her name was Emily. He was saying M for Michelle. I closed my eyes and shook my head. How stupid could I be?

He handed the locket to me. "Open it."

I opened it and took out the small photograph of my mother and me. It was old and cracked, but I recognized it because we had one at Proctor House. "Just because you have the photo from our mantel doesn't mean you're my father."

"Yes it does. I took this when you were a baby, about a week before I knew I had to leave. There was no way I was going to leave the two of you without at least something to remember you by."

I stood up. This was all too much for me to deal with. "I need some tea."

I took a deep breath as I walked out to the shop floor. What was going on with the men in my life? All I needed now was for Liam to drop a bombshell of a revelation on me. Maybe tomorrow, because I couldn't take more today. My mother had made rose hip and lemon tea this morning. I'd have preferred something that packed more of a punch, but this would have to do. I poured myself a mug and leaned against the counter.

I took a sip and tried to calm my racing thoughts. I had so many questions, but those took a back seat to how angry I felt. Was he ever going to tell me he was my father? If he hadn't run into my mother today, would he have continued watching me without saying anything? I put my cup down on the counter, trying not to slam it. It wasn't fair—he'd had the chance over the past few months to get to know me, to watch me without letting me know who he was. Without letting me get to know him as my father.

Tea sloshed over the side of my cup as I grabbed it. We were going to have it out in my office, and they both had a lot to answer for.

I sat back in my chair and tried not to spill any more tea.

"Honey," my mother started, "I know you must have a lot of questions, and we want to answer them all. We need to start by saying you can't tell anyone who Alex is."

"No one? Not even Thea and Delia?" The three of us didn't keep secrets from each other.

She shook her head. "Not for now. I promise it won't be long until you can tell them everything. But you have to consider how they'll feel. Your father is back and theirs aren't. We'll have to be gentle."

She was right but, on the other hand, I knew how excited they'd be for me. "I'll keep the secret for now. But one look at either of you and everyone will know something is up." I looked at Alex—my father. That was going to take some getting used to. "Explain yourself. I want to know exactly why you left us, and why I should ever speak to you again, now that I know who you are and how comfortable you were with deceiving me."

He rubbed his face and looked at my mother. "I knew you'd raise a strong girl."

I wasn't feeling very strong right now. Angry, sure. On the verge of crying for everything I'd lost that had been so close to me for perhaps all my life. "How long have you been in town?"

The three of us were surprised at the anger in my voice. "I'd only been in town for about a week before we met. Before that, I hadn't been in the country since I left Proctor House."

At least he had that going for him. "Why did you abandon us?"

"When you were a baby, I was approached by the fraternity, and they insisted I join them. I put them off for as long as possible, but I knew I'd have to leave. I couldn't join them, and I couldn't continue to evade them. At some point, they would use your mother, or you, as bait to force me to join. So I ran."

"And where were you? Did you never want to send us a message to let us know you were safe?" I asked.

"We decided not to do that," my mother said. "It was safer for us all to break contact and never speak again."

I shifted in my seat. "But it was so hard on you. He should have known that."

"Yes, it was hard on me, on us, but it was much harder on him. We had each other, and the rest of the family. Alex had nothing."

He'd been gone for almost my entire life. I found it hard to believe he'd been alone all that time. "You don't know what he's done in the last twenty years."

She sighed. "I do. We've spent the day talking, and I know there hasn't been a single day he hasn't thought about us, hasn't put our safety above everything else he did, or wanted to do."

I glared at my father. "No second family wherever it was you were hiding all this time?"

He shook his head. "Isabella, of course not. You are my family and, even though I thought I'd never see either of you again, my heart belongs to you and your mother."

The sincerity in his voice made my mother cry, which then set me off. Once we collected ourselves, I had one more question. "So now what?"

My mother wiped tears off her cheeks. "Now we behave like we always have."

"Forever?" I asked.

"No," my father said, "just until I'm sure the family is safe."

The door chime rang and my mother jumped up. "Remember, keep the secret."

We heard her greet Mrs. Kapanga as she closed the office door.

"I gave your wedding ring away," I confessed.

He looked confused. "To who?"

"I gave it to Palmer. The family collaborated to turn it into a talisman to keep him safe. He was running into more trouble with the fraternity, and we were worried we wouldn't be able to protect him all the time. I wanted to make a new one now that we've broken up, because I don't want him to keep the family heirloom."

He thought for a moment. "Let him keep it for now. There may be a time soon when he won't need it anymore."

I couldn't see that happening, but it would make life a lot easier if we didn't need to make him a new charm. "Do you know where Thea's and Delia's fathers are? Or even why they left?"

"I can't tell you everything, but I'll share what I can. Thea's father doesn't have a shred of magic in him. Your Aunt Lily thought she had to tell him about her talents when she got pregnant. She said she didn't want to start a life with him based on a lie. He freaked out and left her."

This tallied with what I'd heard in the past. "But where did he go? Did he go with you?"

"I'm not sure I should say more. This is between him and Lily, and Thea."

"Okay then, what about Delia's father? What can you tell me about him?"

I wasn't expecting much, but he gave me more details about him. "His name is Calvin. He was a witch and was getting pressure from the fraternity like I was." He sighed. "They seem to think every man should want to join the fraternity and were genuinely confused when we didn't."

I had a thought about my cousins and myself. Two of us had witches for a father and one of us didn't. But I'd never say Thea had less ability than Delia or me. I tucked that thought away for a time when I wasn't so busy.

My father continued. "Of course we didn't want to join, but Calvin waited too long to run. He loved Nadia and Delia and couldn't face the idea of leaving them. In the end they caught him and forced him to work with them."

"No," I whispered. I couldn't imagine the horror of being forced to do their bidding. "Does the sorority know? We can save him like we saved Jameson's family. Let me talk to Hope."

He stood up. "I wish it was that simple. It's been decades, and he's not the same man he was. It may be too late for him to go back to having a family. I've got to go back outside. I've been in here too long already, and we don't know who might be watching."

I stood and held my arms out. I wanted to hug him, but he shook his head. "Nothing can change, not until we've destroyed the fraternity. If they knew I was back in town, they'd do their best to make sure I could never break free from them."

    I nodded, even though it broke my heart. Someday we'd be a family again, but not today.

Chapter 12

After the day my mother and I had, we went to the Rusty Pigeon after work. I told her about the drink Kate and I had—the one with the Choco Taco on top of it and frosting around the rim of the glass—and she couldn't believe it. I had to point it out when someone ordered it. We decided a glass of wine was all we could deal with that night.

We sat in a quiet corner and stared at each other for a moment. After I cast a silencing spell so no one could hear us, I said, "I suppose I should be happy, and I am, but I can't help thinking what about Thea and Delia? All our lives we've been the same—living at Proctor House with our mothers. Now suddenly, I'm different."

My mother squeezed my hand. "You've been different for a while now. You were the first to move out in two generations, and you may be the only one who does. As far as I know, you're the only member of the family ever in the sorority, and it's been a long time since any of us has had a familiar."

I took a sip of my Riesling. "I'm different enough as it is. I don't want to be more different."

"I wish there was something I could do, but I can't. It's up to you to decide you're unique, special, talented, and whatever else you think you are. You're all those things, but until you decide you are . . . you're just going to feel like the ugly duckling instead of the amazing woman you've become."

I sighed. I knew this was true, but that didn't make it any easier to live with. At least not now. "Do you think he'll ever be able to come back?"

My mother's eyes shone with tears. "I hope so. Even though he's been gone for so long, by the time we were done talking, it felt like we'd never been apart. We have so much to catch up on, but in my heart he's still the same man I fell in love with, and I could easily fall back into our old life together."

I wanted that. She deserved to be with the man she loved, and who still loved her all this time later. And I wanted that. I had him more in my life than she did and knowing he was my father, it wasn't enough. "I'll do everything I can, mom."

I looked at my watch, surprised to see it was seven o'clock. "That's weird. I haven't heard anything from Jameson yet. He threatened me with extra training until I caught up to wherever he thinks I should be."

My mother frowned. "Maybe he's busy with the kittens. They can tire anyone out."

I stood up. "Let's go back to the house. Maybe we'll find him there and, for once, I'll be prepared to work before he is." I doubted that would happen, but I had hope. Because if he wasn't busy with Jessamin and Jules, something bad was going on. She must have been worried, too, because she led me to the bathroom, then teleported us to Proctor House.

We appeared in the front hallway, expecting the kitchen to be crowded with the rest of the family. I dropped my mother's hand and sent out a message to Jameson. *Jameson, where are you?*

He didn't answer me immediately. Where would he have gotten off to?

The kitchen was full with the rest of the family. "There you are. I was wondering if the two of you were going to be home for dinner or not," Aunt Nadia said.

"Has anyone seen Jameson?" I asked.

They all shook their heads. "Now that you mention it, I haven't seen the kittens all afternoon either," Delia said.

"I'll go check upstairs. Maybe they're asleep," Thea offered.

Grandma looked at my mother. "Michelle, what's going on?"

I looked at Grandma, then my mother, and I knew our secret would come out over dinner. My mother did not have a poker face and, in light of such happy news, I didn't blame her.

"Let's wait until Thea gets back," she stalled.

I tried to take the pressure off her. "Dinner smells great, Aunt Nadia. Chicken tagine?"

"With beet salad, roasted carrots, and fresh pita," she said, without taking her eyes off my mother.

"No kittens upstairs," Thea said when she returned.

Delia frowned. "And they're not answering me, either."

Strange, but not too worrying since the three cats were most likely together. "Let's get dinner on the table, I'm starving," I said, still trying to shield my mother from Grandma's questions.

"You girls do that while Michelle tells us what she's hiding," Grandma insisted.

I looked at her and shrugged. I wasn't sure how Alex expected us to keep this big a secret from the family.

My mother sat down and got to the heart of the matter. "I'll tell you, but it stays in the family. Alex is back in town. He's been watching over Isabella."

Aunt Nadia dropped an empty serving platter and it shattered on the floor. I looked to her, stunned by how pale her complexion had gone. "Here, sit down," I said, guiding her to a chair.

"What about Calvin?" Aunt Nadia whispered.

My mother shook her head. "No word."

"And my father?" Thea asked.

"Alex wouldn't talk about him," I said, wishing I had any information on her father I could share with her.

My cousins sat and held hands. I could see them struggling with conflicting emotions. They were happy for me, but at the same time felt the loss of their own fathers.

"So why isn't he here?" Grandma asked. "Does he expect me to find him myself? I told that boy when he left that he'd have to answer to me if he set foot in my town again."

"Mother, stop. He's been looking out for Isabella for months now and when he thinks it's safe, he'll come back. For now, just let him do what he thinks is best. He says the fraternity hasn't forgotten him."

I looked to Aunt Lily, who was sitting silently and wringing her hands. I didn't know what to say. I wasn't prepared for the depth of sadness my aunts and cousins felt knowing my father had come back, but the other two men in our family hadn't.

Before I could say any more, we all heard cats meowing in the living room. Many cats—not just our three. "What in the world?" Grandma asked.

My cat walked in and fell to the floor. "Jameson!" I rushed to him and started checking him for injuries. Other than singed fur and a burn on one of his paws, he looked okay.

"Let me take a look at him. You go see what that racket is in the other room," Grandma said.

I didn't want to leave him, but in an emergency, Grandma could command us to do anything—no magic involved, just determination.

Thea, Delia, and I walked to the living room and were astonished. There were forty cats, seven dogs, three ravens, more mice than I could count, and a few other animals scurrying around and over the furniture.

Jessamin and Jules ran to my cousins. Not for the first time, I wished I could hear what they were saying instead of having to wait for my cousins to tell me what was happening.

Delia picked her cat up, cradling her gently. "They were in California, raiding as many fraternity locations as possible to set their enslaved familiars free. They had a safe location picked out, but it was compromised so they came here."

I ran back to the kitchen. "We're going to need stronger wards, I think."

Jameson sat up, looking much better. *I took care of that before we left. Just in case.*

The aunts were already working on the wards, but looked confused. "Jameson said he took care of that before he left. We've got a room full of liberated fraternity familiars, and I'm not sure what we should do about it."

Everyone followed me back to the living room. "Oh, bats!" my mother said. "We can't have this many animals in the house."

Jameson jumped on the back of the couch and began to speak so everyone could hear him. "Attention, familiars! We will be staying here for the evening. I remind you that the Proctor witches are our hosts, and you will treat them, and their home, gently. This means no clawing furniture, no chewing through cords, no running around or chasing each other. Is that clear? These witches are not like your captors, so don't treat them, or their home, poorly."

The animals slowed down as he was talking and, by the time he was done, each was sitting still. "Good. I don't know how long we'll stay here, but we'll head out as soon as it's safe."

I rolled my eyes. What were we going to do with all these animals, some of whom were natural predators of others? "Can I talk to you in the other room?" I asked Jameson.

He surveyed the room before jumping off the couch. *Of course*.

I squinted at him as he walked out of the living room. Of course? He was never that polite or amenable to me. Something was up. I took a seat in front of him in the dining room. "What in the seven realms is going on here?"

We were ambushed at the safe house I'd found, so we had to fall back to our second location.

He didn't even scratch the surface of my questions. The more I thought, the more worried I was. "What are we going to do with them? Don't you think the fraternity will check here next? How are we going to hold them all off?" Sure, we'd fought off some of the fraternity in the past, but it looked like Jameson had taken over fifty of their familiars, and they'd stop at nothing to get them back.

Yes, they'll come here next. But the wards are as strong as I could make them, and each of these familiars is willing to fight to keep their freedom.

And each of them knows their former witch's weaknesses. I'm confident we'll win any battle.

I hadn't thought of that. "You'll lead them? I presume they'll listen to you, right?" A loud bark drew our attention to the living room. I sighed. It was going to be a long night.

I can keep them in line. You'll have to stay here tonight, maybe tomorrow.

I wasn't going to argue about that, because I was sure the fraternity would come for their familiars as soon as possible. "Okay. I'll fill in the family, you go keep the peace in there."

My family had moved back into the kitchen and they were arguing. "I'm sure I can find enough food to feed them all," Aunt Nadia said.

"But we shouldn't have to," Grandma countered. "If he'd asked, or at least had the courtesy to tell us his plans, we could have been prepared. But now we've got a zoo, and I'm not sure how long they'll behave."

"Okay," I said loudly. "Here's the thing. They came to us for sanctuary. I'm not sure whether our laws for sanctuary apply to familiars, but for all the help Jameson has been to the family, and the sorority, I say we owe him."

"Yes, but for how long?" Aunt Lily asked.

I pursed my lips. "No way to know, but I'd bet it won't be more than a day. He just stole their familiars, so they'll want to take them back as soon as possible. And before you get all upset, we've got a lot going for us. First, the fraternity is weaker without their familiars. Second, each animal knows its former witch's weaknesses and can exploit them. Third, there are now more of us than fraternity members coming for their familiars, so it's not an even battle. As long as we keep our wits, we'll win."

Thea nodded. "Makes sense. All we need is a strong cloaking spell that will hide anyone who comes close to the house. We can't let the neighbors see what's going to happen, though."

"Michelle and Lily, come help me with that. Nadia, you'd better get to feeding everyone here. We're going to need all the strength we can muster," Grandma said.

A loud rap on the kitchen door startled me. "Isabella, open up!"

I looked to Thea and Delia. "It's my father."

Aunt Nadia opened the door but didn't let him in. "Alex? Is it you?"

He held his arms out wide and turned in a circle. When he faced her again, she let him in.

"It's really him, no glamour, no spells," Aunt Nadia said.

"What are you—" I started.

"I'm here because the fraternity is on its way, and you're going to need all the help you can get."

Chapter 13

It didn't take us long to get organized. The first thing I did was alert the sorority, who all appeared within minutes. I suspect the thought of getting a familiar spurred Claire and Helen to be on their best behavior. The sorority was designed to keep the fraternity at bay, so we all were ready to work together.

The Proctor witches took responsibility for keeping the neighbors from knowing anything that was going on. We'd set up a series of spells to make the neighborhood appear quiet and peaceful, no matter what was going on. First a cloaking spell to keep everything hidden, then a spell that showed Proctor House dark and quiet.

The rescued familiars were going to focus on their former witches, hitting them at all their weakest points. The sorority would take on all other fraternity members with the exception of their leader, Jake Forster. Hope was our general—making sure we worked together and didn't have gaps in our defenses.

"Are you sure you can handle Jake on your own?" I asked my father.

He grinned. "Of course I can. He'll be distracted trying to oversee the entire fight, and that's when I'll get him."

Palmer called and distracted me from watching for the fraternity. "I was wondering—and don't laugh—but is there any way you can find suspects with a spell? I'm at a dead end here, and I'm not sure I've got anywhere to go with this case."

This didn't sound like the Palmer I knew. "No . . . I don't think there's a spell for that. What's going on? You usually have plenty of theories for a case."

He sighed. "I read through Bethany's will. She left everything to charity. I can't see the Visiting Nurses or the Meals on Wheels people killing her for the inheritance. And I don't buy Andrew or Omar as killers."

Andrew was not going to like this. He'd probably contest the will, but Palmer was right, he didn't have a motive. "I agree. But what about someone else? Did she have a financial manager?"

"Not that I could tell. All her files were stolen, but Andrew might know. I'll ask him in the morning. What are you up to tonight? Training with Jameson?"

That was a close enough guess, and I didn't want him to rush over and get in the way. "Yeah. We'll be at it all night."

He laughed. "Okay then. Make sure he lets you sleep and I'll see you tomorrow."

We hung up and I wasn't sure where to go. Did I work with my family to protect our house? Did I go with the sorority to fight off the fraternity? Or should I go with my father, who seemed to be alone and probably needed help, or at least someone to watch his back. And what about the animals? Should I do something with them?

Hope barked my name. She must be anxious to use that tone on me. "You start with your family, but when the fighting starts, you come to me. Your offensive magic is weak, and you'll learn by working with us."

Weak? How about nonexistent? My family had gathered in the kitchen, the heart of the home, to create a cloaking spell large enough to cover the house, the yard, and the road. We needed to go right up to the property line of each of our neighbors, but not cross over to their yards. If we did, and someone decided to check out their back fence, for instance, they might see the upcoming battle because they'd be in the cloaking shield's perimeter.

By eight o'clock we had the cloaking spell up and started bolstering our defenses. The wards laid on the house over the centuries had seeped into the wood, magically speaking, and a quick refresh was all we needed to keep any day-to-day threats from bothering us. But if the expected swarm of fraternity members appeared tonight, we would need substantially stronger defenses.

We layered spells of confusion, pain, fear, forgetfulness, hallucination, and anything else we could think of that would slow down or stop the fraternity members from getting closer to us. We didn't just lay them over the house, either. We staggered them throughout the yard so they wouldn't be able to predict when they'd be hit by another spell.

As we reinforced the last spell at ten o'clock, a group of very loud people walked past the house, sending us into a panic. Clouds blocked the full moon and I couldn't see who they were, or how many. Some of the older witches probably could, but I had no idea. Was this the attack we were waiting for? The animals crowded around the windows Jameson assigned them, sorority witches behind them. My father was on the top floor where he could see at least half the battle at once.

Wait, Hope commanded us telepathically. *We don't know if they are fraternity or not.*

I held my breath and put all my will into the hallucination spell I was casting, determined no one would cross my spell.

False alarm. They had no magic at all, Grandma told us all.

I took a deep breath and rolled my shoulders to release the tension I'd gathered there in the short time we waited. If I was this tense now, how would I be once the actual battle started?

"Girls, if you don't breathe during a fight, you're going to lose," Grandma said.

We were prepared to keep vigil all night, but only had to wait another two hours. At midnight, wind blew the clouds out of the sky and the full moon illuminated our yard. The animals started getting restless, shifting positions and pacing through the house. I rushed into the living room. "Jameson, what's happening? Why are they so restless?"

The animals can feel their former witches coming close. They're moving to where they can best intercept them.

Hope called out to us all. "Get ready! They're almost here."

I rushed back to my family, feeling guilty for leaving them. "Are you okay?" I asked them.

My mother nodded. "We can hold it from here. Go back to Hope."

I hesitated, not wanting to leave them. And honestly, not wanting to fight. Defense suited me better.

"Go," Grandma commanded.

Hope was in the living room, staring out at the front yard. I followed her gaze and watched in amazement as fraternity witches teleported themselves into our cloaking spell. Most stayed toward the edge of the field, but the few who had appeared closer to the house immediately felt the effects of our defensive spells.

Flame shot toward the house from a dozen witches, but as they walked forward, they faltered, slowed by our spells. Several witches stepped back, and it was obvious when they left the range of the spell they were feeling.

"Pay attention, Isabella," Hope snapped at me.

I looked at her, then back to the yard. "What do you want me to do?"

"As I was saying," she huffed, "choose one person and focus your magic on him. Drive him into one of the traps. I've got the guy in the red sweatshirt. See him?"

I saw him, and he was fighting Hope as much as he could, but he was slowly moving to our left. I didn't see any traps there, so I had no idea what she was doing. "I see him. Is there a trap nearby?"

"He's about five feet from one. It looks like a hallucination trap."

Oh! Those traps. "I was thinking physical traps. I can't see them, so how do I know where to push the witch I pick?"

Hope gave her guy one large shove into the hallucination trap. He screamed and began to slap at his skin, then rolled on the ground. "Heh, he thinks he's on fire." She turned to me. "What do you mean you can't see the traps?"

"I can only see magic when Thea, Delia, and I work together to find it."

She held her hand out to me. "Here, I'll show you."

I took her hand and gaped at the glowing, colorful ribbons of light coming from each witch and familiar. I'd never seen magic look so vibrant with my cousins.

"Look at the yard. Do you see what to do now?" Hope asked as the magic coming from her tried to encircle another witch on the lawn.

The fraternity realized their flame wasn't breaching our defenses and switched to a new tactic. Piles of rocks appeared beside each fraternity witch and they began hurling them toward the house. They needed magic, because each rock was too large to pick up, much less throw, without it.

I saw the wards on the house wobble as a few stones hit. "Should I go back to the kitchen?" I asked.

"No. They've got it. Focus on the magic outside and how it feels. Now find someone to confront and make him leave us alone."

I looked outside and found a witch who wasn't already engaged. I snaked my magic along the ground and behind him. I made my magic grab his hair and pull him into the trap behind him—into a confusion spell. The stone he'd lifted fell and landed at his feet. "How do I keep him here?" I asked, panting from the energy I'd used just to get him there.

"Think of something like a tent stake. Ram it into the ground and tie your magic to it, and to him. It will take him several minutes to get free, if he can work through the spell," Hope said.

A tent stake? Not very witchy, but I did what she said and he stayed where I put him. I looked around to choose another target when I noticed some of the witches were kneeling with their hands behind their backs, no magic coming from them at all. "Hope, what's happening? Are they giving up?"

"That's your father's work. I didn't think he'd be able to bring down so many. Go see if you can help him, he must be getting exhausted."

I let go of Hope's hand and the magic swirling around me dimmed, but didn't disappear. I ran upstairs to see my father, sweating and trembling. I pulled a chair behind him. "Can you sit?"

Without breaking contact with the witch he was fighting, he slowly lowered himself into the chair. I followed the line of his magic and saw it enveloping Forster. "Tell me what to do," I said.

"Take my hand and lend me your strength. I don't think I can beat him without help."

I took his hand and called to my mother. *Hey, can you come help us? Alex is fighting Forster, and I'm not sure how it's going to go.*

She didn't bother to answer, just appeared beside us. She placed her hand under his and the three of us focused on our target. Alex stopped shaking, and the magic around Forster began to glow brighter and pulse. I felt something crack outside and Forster began to kneel. He stopped and forced himself back up again.

My father groaned. I wished I knew how to loan him more of my strength, but I was already exhausted. "Get him, Dad," I whispered as I sat on the floor, not breaking contact with him.

With one final surge of magic, Forster slammed to the ground. The three of us gasped, exhausted. *Close the cordon, Hope*. I heard my father say.

I watched as a wall of magic began forcing everyone outside into the front yard and into a decreasing circle, and then they vanished.

I sagged against the chair. "Did they just escape?" I asked, worried we'd lost them.

"No," my mother reassured me as she sat on the other arm of the chair. "If all went well, they're in Sewall. The judge is going to have his work cut out for him going through all those cases."

Sasha slowly climbed the stairs and joined us. "Good work, you three." She handed us each a water bottle. "It's not water. You need to get your strength back, and this is the fastest way to do it. My advice is to drink it fast and eat something right after to kill the taste."

I looked from her to my parents, who hadn't stopped holding hands.

"Thanks. We'll be downstairs in a minute," my mother said. She opened my father's bottle and handed it to him. "I know you hate this, but drink it anyway."

He took one large gulp and grimaced. "Brimstone, that's gross. You'd think someone would come up with a better flavor by now."

I opened mine, determined to drink it all at once. I almost did, but the flavor was most like the inside of an unwashed garbage truck and my body rebelled. I forced myself to swallow what was in my mouth, then looked at the bottle. One large sip to go. I could do it, because I was already feeling stronger. I choked the last of it down, then checked my parents had done the same. I could tell they had, because they were standing. One minute ago, none of us could have stood.

They helped me up and hugged me. I sank into the hug, my first two-parent hug that I could remember, and basked in their love.

And then I burped. "Oh, moldy bat wings. It's worse now." I put my hand over my mouth, just in case any tried to come back up.

"Food helps, and I'm sure Nadia's got something in the kitchen," my father said.

Chapter 14

My father was right. Aunt Nadia had food out and ready for us, even as some people were still choking down their potions. She pulled out a chair for my father and took his arm. "Here, Alex. Let me help you to a chair."

"Nadia, I'm fine," he said. But I noticed he didn't stand back up again.

Aunt Lily handed me a glass of milk. "Here, drink this. It'll help your stomach."

I wasn't sure what it was about the milk, but it removed all traces of that vile potion from my mouth. "Wow, thanks." I sat between my parents and surveyed the room. "Are the animals okay?" I asked.

"They are. They can't have the potion, so they're all fast asleep. We won't hear from them until tomorrow," Hope said.

The kitchen wasn't large enough to seat the family and the sorority, so Aunt Nadia moved us all to the blue dining room, where she'd laid out a feast of food, all with cheese. I helped myself to a grilled cheese sandwich and another glass of milk.

Once I'd finished half my sandwich and my father had demolished a plate of lasagna, I asked him, "What were you doing to them?"

He looked to me, sadness in his eyes. "I took their power from them."

I gasped. That was the kind of magic we'd always been warned to stay away from. "You can do that? How? Why? Where did you learn that kind of evil magic?"

"Isabella," my mother said.

My father shushed her. "It's okay, M. She's worried, and rightly so. I had to learn these kind of spells to survive. If I hadn't, you'd have been fighting me out there."

Tears gathered in my eyes. "But you stole their power."

He shook his head. "I didn't. I returned it back to the earth. I put it into your gardens, and let's just say you won't have much work to do there for a very long time."

"Will they ever get their power back?" I asked.

He shook his head. "No. But there were so many of them that I might have missed some of their minor abilities. So they're still witches, just with no useful talents."

I wished that didn't need to happen, and I felt sorry for them. I couldn't imagine my life without magic.

"Don't feel too sorry for them, Isabella," Grandma said. "They were coming for us and, had they won, they wouldn't have been half as kind to us."

I shuddered, then yawned. "I'm going to sleep. Palmer is going to need me in the morning."

My parents kissed me goodnight, and I went upstairs, Thea and Delia joining me.

"Did he say anything about my father?" Delia asked.

I shook my head. "He didn't say anything to me. I don't even know if he was out in the yard. Do you think that was every single fraternity member? Maybe some didn't show up."

She shrugged. "I'm afraid to ask."

Thea and I hugged her. "I can ask him tomorrow, if you want," I offered.

Delia started to cry. "I don't know. No, don't ask. There's no answer that will make me happy."

My heart broke for her. I glanced at Thea, and she didn't look very happy either. "At least your father has a reason to not be here. Mine just left because he had stupid prejudices he didn't love my mother or me enough to work through."

We all got a slow start the next morning. By the time I'd made it to the kitchen, only Grandma, Aunt Nadia, and Thea were there. Everyone else, including all the familiars, were still asleep. I'd just poured myself a second large mug of coffee when there was a knock on the door. All our protective and disguise spells were still up, so I was surprised anyone could have actually made it to the door. I looked out the window to see Palmer waiting for me.

"I altered the spells so Palmer's ring would let him inside the disguise spell," Grandma said. "Are you going to let him in or keep him standing there?"

I opened the door and gave him a tired smile.

"What happened here last night, and why didn't I hear anything about it?" he asked

"You weren't working last night, were you? Tell me you don't spend all your off time listening to the scanner."

"No. I don't need to. Dispatch calls me if anything happens to your apartment, this house, or to anyone named Proctor."

I shook my head and sat back down. "I'm not sure you'd believe it if I told you."

Aunt Nadia placed a platter of waffles between us. "Help yourself, Detective. It's going to take her a while to tell you everything."

He looked at his phone. "We've got a search warrant to execute in about an hour, so can I get the short version?"

My eyes widened. "What are you searching for, and can I come?"

He took two waffles from the platter and put them on the plate Thea put in front of him. "I found her lawyer, and his firm handled her finances too." He paused and looked at the strawberries and maple syrup. "Berries or syrup?"

"I'm coming with you, and I'm going half and half—why choose just one?" I said, pouring maple syrup on half my waffle.

He followed my lead and started eating. After two bites, he paused to ask, "Okay, so what happened? It looks like you had a frat party out there."

I sighed, exhausted just thinking about it. "Yesterday, Jameson liberated over fifty fraternity familiars who were being held against their will. He'd set up a safe house, but it was compromised, so they all came here."

"You have fifty cats in the house?" he asked, eyes wide. He was probably envisioning fifty snarky Jameson clones.

"Not just cats. We've also got dogs, birds, and mice. They're still asleep though. The fraternity came around midnight to reclaim the animals, and we fought them off. That's the frat party look outside. None of the neighbors can see what you saw, though. To them, the house looks like it always does."

Palmer poured himself a cup of coffee. "You fought off the fraternity? Just the seven of you?"

I chuckled. "No, we had the sorority and the animals helping. And someone you probably ought to meet. Well, not meet, because you've met him before, but you should be reintroduced to my father."

He looked confused. "I've met your father? When?"

As if he'd been listening at the door, my father walked in, a giant smile on his face. "Detective Palmer, it's nice to see you again." He held his hand out while Palmer stared at him in disbelief.

After a moment, Palmer shook his hand. "You're her father?" He looked to me, confused. "Why didn't you recognize him?"

I hadn't seen my father since I was very young and, even though I'd seen photos of him, I'd never recognized him as the man in the photos. "I never expected to see him, and I stopped looking for his face in crowds years ago."

Palmer took a bite of waffle. "I guess I don't have to worry about why you were guarding Isabella anymore. It's good to meet you, sir. I hope you'll be staying in Portsmouth for a while."

My father sat next to me and put his arm around my shoulder. He pulled me close and kissed me on the top of my head. I leaned into him and closed my eyes. For years, this was all I'd hoped for and he was finally here. "I plan to stay forever," he said.

I opened my eyes and smiled up at him. Our relationship wasn't the usual father–daughter one and, even though I hadn't had a chance to get to know him as a member of my family, I already trusted him because he'd been watching out for me for months.

"So you all beat down the fraternity last night. When do you expect they'll return?" Palmer asked.

"We did more than beat them down. The sorority captured most of them and mass teleported them to Sewall. You won't have to worry about them for a very long time," my father explained.

"You're being modest," I said. "We couldn't have done it if you hadn't stripped power from Forster and several other fraternity members first."

Palmer dropped his fork. "Forster isn't a witch anymore?"

I wasn't sure if that was technically correct. What did one call a witch whose powers had been taken away? And for that matter, I wasn't even sure all his powers were gone. All I could tell was that his ability to cast spells was gone.

"I can explain that in more detail," Alex said. "The spell I cast strips a witch of his ability to cast spells, create potions, or perform any of the other major magics. It's possible he'll be able to find some small abilities he'll still be able to do, but he'll never be a threat to anyone again."

Palmer picked up his fork and stabbed a strawberry. "What's to prevent someone from taking his place and leading the fraternity?"

My mother walked into the kitchen and kissed my father, then me. "Good morning, you two."

My father stood and held his seat out for her. "Let me get you breakfast, M."

I hadn't been able to watch my parents together for very long yesterday, and last night we were too focused on the fraternity, but now I was happy to see them looking at each other, still in love after such a long separation.

As my father prepared a plate for my mother, he continued to explain. "I hit the top seven members of the fraternity before I couldn't go on. They'll be tried in Sewall, then sent to prisons around the country. There may be a few members who weren't here last night that may try to recreate the group. I'm sure the sorority will keep an eye on them."

"Just like that? The fraternity is gone?" Palmer asked incredulously.

I frowned. "Possibly, but like Alex said, the sorority will keep watch on them, just in case." I wondered if, now that it would be easy to escape, Delia's father could come home too. I didn't want to ask in front of the family, in case the answer was no. But I still hoped. "What's this search warrant you've got?" I asked again.

"It's for the financial records for the Fancy Tart, and for Bethany's private finances. She ran everything through her lawyer, Shrewsbury."

I made a face. "He tried to talk me into using him, but I didn't like how I felt with him. Something was off, and so I said I'd think about it but never went back to him. I think he just didn't want to lose control over Trina's estate. If you give me five minutes, I'll be ready to go."

Chapter 15

Palmer ushered me out the door after I finished getting ready. The front yard looked worse in the daylight, and I felt bad for the rest of the family who would spend the day cleaning it up and healing the damaged plants. I walked down to the huge chestnut tree at the end of the driveway and put my hand on the trunk. "Sorry you had to deal with all that last night," I whispered to it.

Palmer said nothing until we got into the car. Before he pressed the ignition button, he turned to me. "Your father? Really?"

I grinned. "Yes. I can't believe he's back. And I like him. I mean, I liked him before I knew who he was too, but now . . ."

"Your family is sure it's not some sort of spell, or trick, right? I've seen spells that make you look like someone else."

"Aunt Nadia checked him out last night before she let him into the house. He's really who he says he is."

Palmer started the car. "Then I don't understand why he was sleeping in a tent next to your greenhouse, or why he was living out on the streets for months before that. Why not go to Proctor House and ask your mother to take him back?"

"He was afraid of the fraternity. They got to Delia's father and he couldn't escape. It wasn't until last night, when the fraternity was weak because they had lost so many of their familiars, that he thought we could take them on and win."

Palmer parked in front of Shrewsbury's law firm. "I'm glad he's back, and your mother looks very happy. You do too. I hope this all works out for your family."

He opened his door. "But now, to work. I don't expect problems but, if he's reluctant to answer questions, I know you can charm him."

I smiled. I still had no idea where my ability to make people want to talk to me came from. It didn't feel like magic to me, and it wasn't something I did intentionally. Once, Palmer said I'd make a good detective, so maybe it was just a natural talent. "You got it. Are you expecting to see anything suspicious in her financials?"

"Not sure but, if you have a bad feeling about him, I'm willing to trust your instinct."

We walked into his office and were greeted by the firm's receptionist. "Welcome to Shrewsbury and Associates. How can I help you?"

"Good morning. We need to speak to Mr. Shrewsbury," Palmer said.

The receptionist frowned. "I'm afraid he's in meetings all day. Could I take a message for you and have him call you back as soon as he can?"

Palmer took the warrant from his jacket pocket. "No. I wanted to speak to him as a courtesy. I can have officers here going through all the files in the office until they find what I need." He pulled out his phone and started dialing.

"I'm sure that won't be necessary," she said hastily. "Let me interrupt him for a moment." She took the warrant from Palmer and hurried into the inner office. She didn't knock, so I doubted he was even in a meeting.

Shrewsbury walked out of the office, all smiles. "Detective Palmer, how good to see you. You want to see the financials for Mrs. Swift?" He glanced at his watch. "I'm sure I can have those for you by the close of business on Friday."

Today was Tuesday, why would he need four days to assemble files that should be in a folder somewhere? Whether the files were electronic or paper, it should only take him a few minutes to assemble them. What was he trying to hide?

Palmer smiled, but there was no warmth behind his eyes. "I wouldn't want to be a bother. As I told your receptionist, I can get a team in here to find the files. I'm sure they wouldn't take more than a day or two to go through everything. They'd be very thorough."

I wondered, could Palmer do that? The look on Shrewsbury's face said he might, and he wasn't taking a chance of someone going through all his files.

"I'm sure that won't be necessary. I'll have them couriered to your office today."

"No need. We'll wait here," Palmer said, eyeing the chairs in the reception area. I thought if I sank into the comfortable couch I'd be in danger of falling asleep. Maybe the hard wooden chair in the corner would be better for me.

"Eva, please assemble all the records we have for Mrs. Swift," Shrewsbury said. "And while we're waiting, I'd like to talk to Miss Proctor."

I looked at Palmer and he nodded. I wasn't interested in talking to the lawyer I'd already decided not to work with, but now was my chance to get more information out of him. Once we were seated in his office, he began the sales pitch. "I've been keeping an eye on your business, and I'm not sure it's going to stay afloat without some serious financial management in place."

I was pretty sure that was a lie. "What do you mean?"

He folded his hands on his desk. "I've noticed you let your assistant go. To be honest, I think you jumped the gun in terms of taking on additional financial responsibilities. Had you come to me for advice, I could have told you it was a mistake to overextend yourself like that."

Who did he think he was? Not someone who knew anything about the apothecary, that was for sure. "What would you suggest?" I asked, certain I wouldn't take any of his advice.

"I'd suggest you let my firm do an extensive audit of your business and let us make recommendations. In most cases, when a business is overextended like yours is, I suggest pulling back on the wide variety of products and focusing your product line. For example, do you really need an entire wall of tea? Surely people only drink four or five different types. You lose money carrying such a wide variety that doesn't sell very well."

I rolled my eyes. He knew nothing about running an apothecary. "I appreciate your advice, but I think I'll stick it out for a while longer."

"You can't have many more months before you stop taking a salary, if you haven't already," he said.

He almost had me. I almost started telling him how well I was doing. I wanted to explain Mackenzie had moved to Canada and that Omar would replace her very soon. Instead, I stood. "I don't think it will come to that."

I joined Palmer in the lobby and fifteen minutes later, Shrewsbury emerged from his office with a file box and a data stick. "Paper and electronic records for Mrs. Swift's business and personal finances. I'll make myself available if you have any questions."

Palmer took the box. "Thank you. I'm sure our forensic accountant has your number."

"Got anything else for me today?" I asked.

Palmer started the car. "No. Not unless you've got hidden talents as an accountant."

I laughed. "Definitely not. But I'm not as bad as Shrewsbury thinks I am. He tried to tell me the apothecary was going to fail if I didn't hire him. He said he could tell it was doing poorly because I'd had to fire Mackenzie."

"But . . . didn't she move?" Palmer asked.

"Yes, she did. And Omar is starting any day now. But he doesn't know that. He thinks I'm about to start taking no salary to keep the apothecary afloat. Shows how much he knows."

"Where am I dropping you off?" Palmer asked.

"Proctor House. I should help with the cleanup." And my father was there. I wanted to spend as much time with him as I could, in case he had to leave again.

"I'd like to take you to lunch today," he said. "Not for work, just to spend a little time together."

I didn't feel good about that. I still had another date with Liam coming up at some point, and I was looking forward to it. Could it be that Palmer and I weren't made for each other? I wasn't sure anymore.

"I don't think I'll have time. It can be draining to keep the spells up over the whole house for an extended period of time and, even though she wouldn't complain, Grandma looked very tired this morning. Maybe another time?"

The smile on his face fell. "Yeah, uh sure. Some other time."

Chapter 16

We spent the rest of the day cleaning, fixing the gouges in the lawn, and healing the burns on the trees in the yard. By the time night fell, Grandma was able to release the spells they'd kept up.

Hope and Sasha returned after dinner with a surprise for Thea and Delia. Sasha had finally made two new amulets that didn't explode after being used. "They don't even overheat, so I think I've finally got the process figured out."

Hope showed them to us. "Since you are the first witches to wear these amulets, we would usually name them after you. But we can't have two Proctor amulets, so I propose using your first instead of last names."

My cousins eyed the amulets suspiciously. "How certain are you that it won't explode?" Delia asked.

Sasha was quick to reassure them. "Almost a hundred percent."

"Almost?" Thea asked.

"Well, all amulets come with a small amount of risk," Hope said.

This was news to me. I took my amulet off and stared at it. I turned it over, but it seemed the same as always. I squinted at it and tried to telepathically communicate with it, commanding it not to explode on me. It didn't answer. Not that I expected it to.

"Exactly how much risk are we talking about here?" Aunt Lily asked.

"And has Isabella been in danger all this time?" my mother demanded.

Hope raised her hands to settle the family down. "Isabella's not at any risk, unless she tries to do something so horrible the amulet won't allow it. Thea and Delia will have to do some testing on their amulets, but Sasha and I are certain they will be fine."

"I don't think I should allow it," Aunt Nadia said.

I whipped my head around to look at her. She was the aunt least likely to decree anything. For her to say she might not allow it was incredibly out of character for her.

"Does the amulet come with a cost? Will the girls have to join the sorority as well?" Aunt Lily asked.

I hadn't had time to think about that. Having people who liked me in the sorority would be nice, but did I want them in life-threatening situations? They'd both done well holding up the shields last night, but I wasn't sure they were ready for the kind of fighting we had to do sometimes.

And what if all three of us were hurt or killed? That would devastate the family. "I'm not sure it's a good idea either. One dangerous event could take out our entire generation and then there'd be no more Proctor witches."

No one looked happy about that idea.

"But is that likely to happen?" Thea asked. "The fraternity is in shambles, and no one thinks they can come back from last night. We'll have plenty of time to learn and train before we need to worry about anyone dangerous."

She had a point there. Before I could say anything, Delia took an amulet from Hope and slid it over her head. "I accept."

Thea took the other and followed Delia. "Me too."

Hope looked at the two of them, exasperated. "That's not how this was supposed to go. I know Isabella didn't follow tradition, but I was hoping we could get back to it. You were supposed to wait until we were all here to welcome you."

Sasha grinned. "I told you it was a waste of time to plan a whole ceremony. These girls are impetuous, and we'll need to rein them in."

"Part of the ceremony was to initiate you into the sorority as trainees. We have enough full members that we can take our time training you, keeping you safe until you're ready to face whatever takes the place of the fraternity. So I guess I'll skip all the kind words and welcoming phrases and tell you not to use the amulets unless you're with an older witch. Preferably me or Esther, any of your mothers would do if necessary." She paused and took a deep breath. "It is important that you pay close attention to this, girls. Isabella is not a suitable choice here. She needs more training before she's ready to supervise anyone."

"Why? Are you saying the girls are in danger?" Aunt Nadia asked. She reached over to Delia and grabbed the chain. "Take it off, just for now." Aunt Nadia tried to lift the chain over Delia's head, but it wouldn't move.

"Ow! Stop it, mom. It's screaming at me."

We'd all heard an amulet scream before, when Brent Thompson tried to wear my amulet. Only then it had screamed out loud and everyone, or at least every witch, could hear it. At least Delia's amulet was only screaming to her.

Aunt Nadia let go and took a step back. "Okay, you try taking it off."

Slowly, Delia shook her head. "No. It belongs with me."

Hope grabbed Aunt Nadia's arm. "Stop it, Nadia. We just got done telling you the amulets needed to be treated gently and you're trying to yank it off her?"

Aunt Lily's arm dropped. She'd had second thoughts about taking Thea's amulet off. "What can we do to make sure they're safe?"

"Their best bet is to work with their familiars. As the three entities—witch, familiar, and amulet—learn to work together, Thea and Delia will be able to control the amulet's magic."

I didn't understand why I never got this advice. I was sort of an emergency addition to the sorority and maybe there just wasn't time. "Is that something I should do too?"

Jameson and the kittens jumped up on the kitchen table. *Why do you think we train so hard every day? Your amulet was never in danger of exploding, because it's used to working with witches, but having the three of us train together every day is important.*

"Does that mean we can stop working so hard every night? I'd love a full night's sleep once in a while," I said.

He didn't answer me, but looked skeptical.

Jules and Jessamin jumped off the table and walked out of the kitchen, Thea and Delia following behind. Hope and Sasha left and the rest of the family drifted off to other rooms of the house. My parents had gone out for a walk, so I was about to leave for my apartment. I was ready for a quiet night alone.

"Isabella?" Thea called in a trembling voice. "Can you come in here please?"

I followed her voice to the red dining room where she and Delia were staring at the upholstered chair next to the fireplace.

"What's up?" I asked.

Without moving her head, Thea said, "I think these amulets are bad. We can see . . ."

"Don't tell her," Delia whispered. "Isabella, who do you see sitting in the chair?"

There was no one in the chair. "Uh, no one." I took hold of my amulet and tried to make it show me someone in the chair, but had no luck. "Not even with the amulet."

Delia turned to me. "Okay, well, we see Grandpa. He's sitting in his overalls like he's just been working in the garden and Grandma's going to yell at him for getting dirt on the furniture. He's grinning like he's happy to see us."

Oh broomsticks! That wasn't good. Ghosts weren't meant to be seen and, if a witch was seeing them, it meant big trouble. "Are you sure about that?"

My cousins nodded in unison.

"Okay, what do Jules and Jessamin have to say?" I asked, hoping they'd have an answer to what was going on here.

"They ran out," Thea said.

I telepathically called for Jameson, and he appeared instantly. "What's wrong?" he asked, speaking aloud so Thea and Delia could hear him.

"They say Grandpa's ghost is sitting on the chair by the fireplace," I said.

Jameson walked to the chair, sniffing the air as he did. He walked around it and finally jumped onto the arm of the chair. "Yes, he's here. Or at least his ghost is here."

I sat at the table next to my cousins. Ghosts were real? And the children's stories about them trying to steal your power were lies?

"You can see ghosts? Why didn't you tell me this before?"

"They're real, but almost no one can see them so no one cares," Jameson said. "I'd like one of you to take off your amulet, just for a moment. I want to see if it's the reason you can see ghosts."

Delia raised a shaky hand to her necklace. "I'll do it. Hopefully it won't scream at me." As the chain moved over her head, she let out a sigh of relief. "No screaming. And no Grandpa."

"He's still there," Thea said.

"Thea, I want you to talk to him. Let's see if the two of you can communicate," Jameson said.

Thea stood up and walked to the fireplace. "Grandpa," she said shakily, "can you hear me?"

She stood for a minute, then turned back to us, tears running down her face. "Yes, we can talk together. He says staying here has kept him from feeling so lonely. He loves us all and will continue to watch over us."

I rubbed my amulet with my thumb. I wanted to talk to Grandpa, too, but I still couldn't see him.

"Isabella, he says you can talk to him anytime you want, and he'll hear you. He's sad he can't answer you though," Thea said.

That was something, I guess. "Who wants to tell Grandma?"

"Tell Grandma what?" she asked from the doorway. I swear she knew the instant we were talking about her, no matter where she was.

"It looks like the amulets are letting Thea and Delia see ghosts. Jameson doesn't seem worried, and right now they're seeing Grandpa," I said.

"Earl? Are you really there?" Grandma asked, looking at the chair at the head of the dining table.

Delia stood, put her arm around Grandma, and turned her toward the chair

Grandpa was sitting in. "He's in the chair, Grandma."

Grandma took two hesitant steps toward the chair and stopped. "If I talk to him, can he hear me?"

Thea nodded. "Yes. I'll tell you what he says."

"Earl, I've missed you so much. I wish I knew you were here all this time with me."

Thea listened, then said, "He says he hears you whenever you talk to him. He answers you every time, even though you can't hear him." She laughed. "He also says maybe you shouldn't have said such mean things to him when he died. He didn't mean to get sick, you know, and he never wanted to leave you."

Grandma teared up. "You old fool. I was only angry because I wasn't ready to stop loving you yet. I guess I'm still not."

Thea hugged Grandma. "That's from him. He says he hasn't stopped loving you either."

Grandma straightened up. "Okay girls, I need one of those amulets. I'm going to call Hope and get her to bring me one. Earl, you wait right there and soon we'll be able to talk to each other without getting the girls involved."

After Grandma left, Delia put her amulet back on. "I can see him again. Hi, Grandpa."

She smiled as he started talking to her. I felt left out and wondered if I could trade this amulet in for a new one.

Chapter 17

It was time to go home. I needed time to sit and think about everything that had happened over the last day. I wasn't sure what my life would be like anymore. The fraternity was damaged beyond repair, my father was back home, and Grandpa was home and at least able to talk to two of us.

I could have used a week to process all these changes and the emotions they brought up, but I suspected I'd only have one night.

I wished my parents had come back from their walk. Talking things out with them would have helped. I'd have to invite them to my apartment sometime soon because there was so much I wanted to ask them.

Liam hadn't called, and I'd expected to hear from him about another date. I was excited to tell him about everything that had happened since I'd seen him last. He'd understand why seeing Grandpa was maybe not a good thing, even though we were all treating it like it was.

Jameson joined me on the walk home. "Don't even tell me we're training tonight. I'm having a bubble bath and going straight to sleep." I didn't care what he said, I wasn't changing my mind.

<*No training tonight. I came to tell you I have to get the familiars situated in new homes. A large number of them have decided they don't want to work with any witches—good or bad—and just want to run off and follow their animal nature.*

I wasn't sure I blamed them. The treatment they received under the fraternity couldn't have been good, and I knew some had been forcibly restrained for years. They needed time to get used to a life of freedom before they made any choices about their futures. "Do they have to go to a new witch right away? Can't they have some time alone first, and then they can choose who they want to go to?"

They could, but I'm afraid we'll lose too many of them.

I stopped walking. "Okay, you might. But if you have to force them into another situation, how are you different than the fraternity? These are sentient beings, and you can't just force them to do what you want, not unless you intend to use force to make sure they obey you."

He licked his paw and thought about it. *I hate it when my humans are right about things I've overlooked. They'll be safer with a witch, and that's what I was focusing on. But you're right. They have to choose their next steps. Since that's the case, it'll be a week or so before I'm back in town. If you need me, call, but try not to need me.*

I said I'd try to hold everything together until he got back. He walked into an alley and vanished, and I went home. I grabbed my mail and unlocked the inner door of my apartment building.

Mrs. Subramanian opened the door to her apartment and brought me a vase of red and white roses. "These were delivered for you earlier today. I hope you don't mind that I trimmed the stems and put them in water for you. I wasn't sure when you'd be home, and it would have been a shame if they wilted before you had the chance to see them."

I gave her a tired smile. "Of course I don't mind. That was very thoughtful, thank you." I took the card from the flowers and opened it.

<indent> I know you've been too busy to see me, so call when you're available. I don't want to get in the way of your work. </indent>

"Are they from Detective Palmer? He is very much in love with you," she said.

"No, we're not together anymore. These are from a man I went out with a few days ago." I sniffed the roses and was pleased Liam chose some that the scent hadn't been bred out of.

"It must have been a wonderful date, because these are lovely," she said. "It's been a long time since Manit has bought me flowers."

I chose one white and one red and gave them to her. "Here. Keep these for yourself." I'd be as happy with ten roses as I would with a dozen—happier, actually, because I knew she'd also be happy.

"Thank you, Isabella. Maybe Manit will take the hint."

I yawned. "I'm so sorry! It's been a busy few days. Have a good night."

I trudged up the stairs, not even trying to sneak past Bruce's apartment. True to form, he opened the door as I walked by. "Oh, you're back. I've enjoyed the quiet, so make sure you don't disturb me tonight."

I didn't even look at him. I opened my door, placed the flowers on my dining room table and kicked off my shoes. The couch looked inviting, but I knew if I sat there, I'd fall asleep and wake up cold and uncomfortable in the middle of the night. I pulled my phone out of my pocket and called Liam instead.

"Hi, it's me," I said, hoping he'd programmed my name into his phone.

"Oh, hi. I wasn't expecting to hear from you tonight. How are you?" he asked.

I sat on the couch, determined not to fall asleep. "Exhausted. Thank you for the flowers. They're beautiful and are sitting on my dining table. Did your grandmother fill you in on everything going on here?"

"She did. I told her I was going to call you today, and she suggested I wait. When she explained it all, I knew you were going to need a while before you had energy for pretty much anything."

I smiled. It was so nice to talk to someone who knew what a witch's life was like. "True. I'm having an early night and then I need to get back to work first thing in the morning. How about we go out on Thursday? I should be ready for a relaxing dinner by then."

"Thursday it is. I'll text you with details later. I don't want to keep you, so get a good night's sleep and I'll see you soon."

"Thanks, I will."

"And, Isabella, thanks for saving us. You have no idea how afraid a lot of us were of the fraternity."

I almost dropped the phone. No one had ever thanked me for saving them before. "Uh, you're welcome. But you know I didn't do it alone. I had a lot of help."

"I know. But you were there. Thank you."

We hung up and I just stared at my phone. Palmer had thanked me in the past for helping him, but this was different. Liam knew exactly what it took to do what we did, and how hard the fraternity was to take down. Sure, my father cast a lot of the key spells, but we all fought in our own way, with our own skills.

I slept as late as possible and rushed to work the next morning. My parents were there, drinking tea and grinning at each other. "Morning, you two."

They enclosed me in a hug, and I felt some of the sadness of growing up without a father vanish. "Neither of you need to be here today, if you don't want. Why don't you go have a day together."

My father shook his head. "Can't. I want to review the security tapes from last night, and I need to pack up my tent. There's no sense for me to sleep there, now that I've finally returned to Proctor House."

They giggled and I rolled my eyes. "Okay, maybe if the two of you could stop acting like lovesick teenagers? You're going to drive the customers away." I tried on my most professional voice. "This is a business establishment, and I must insist on a level of decorum the two of you don't seem to meet."

We all started laughing. "We'll go, but we'll come back with lunch," my father said. "I want to make sure I spend time with you too."

"Fine, now get out of here. And set the sign to say open for me." It was a few minutes before ten, but that was okay.

They hadn't lit my candle for Trina yet. It had been just over a year since she'd died, and it was amazing how much my life had changed since then. I ran a business, I had my father back, I was so much stronger in my powers than I'd ever expected. I had a familiar and two different men that cared about me. I lit her candle. "Oh, Trina. I wish you were here to see it all. You'd be so proud of me."

The truth was, I was proud of myself.

The door chimes rang, and I looked to see a man in a gray suit standing in the doorway. "Good morning. I'm Jason Sevigny, and I'm with Shrewsbury and Associates. I'm looking for Isabella Proctor."

He didn't look like my usual customer, but it could be hard to tell. "I'm Isabella. Come on in. I'm not interested—"

As he crossed the threshold, he turned into dust.

Chapter 18

What in the seven realms was going on? I sent out an emergency message to my parents, warning them to stay outside.

My parents arrived together. "What's wrong?" my father asked.

"That pile of dust? It was a person just a minute ago. He tried to cross the threshold and that's what happened to him. I don't know what's going on here."

My mother put her hand on the doorjamb. "The wards are intact, but there's another spell here."

My father put his hand on hers. "It's fading, because it was a one-time spell. It was designed to kill the person who walked through the door at exactly ten this morning."

What? But how? "I thought the wards prevented things like this."

My father frowned. "This spell didn't trigger the wards, though I'm not sure why. It was a very complex and subtle spell."

My father stepped over the remains of Mr. Sevigny and survived to make it into the shop. "It's perfectly safe to come in and out now."

"I'm calling Palmer," I said.

Palmer arrived in three minutes. He examined the pile of ash, then took photos. "He just . . ."

"Turned to ash. Instant cremation. It's safe to come in if you want," I said.

He rubbed his face. "How did this happen?"

Before I could explain, my father jumped in. "Last night someone put a spell on the front door. It was a one-time spell designed to kill the person who walked through the door at exactly ten."

"Isabella's almost always here early, so who would want to kill her first customer? How would the murderer even know who would have stepped through the door? It doesn't make any sense."

I shrugged. "His name was Jason Sevigny. He said he worked for Shrewsbury. I started to tell him I wasn't interested in anything his boss had to say, but I didn't get the chance."

Palmer started to pace the room. "How are we going to explain this to his family? It's not like we can tell the truth." He looked at my dad. "Could you tell who cast the spell?"

My dad shook his head. "The spell was fading fast, but I could tell it was expertly cast.

We're looking for a witch who wanted to hurt Isabella and who didn't get caught up in the fight two nights ago."

I sat on the stool behind the counter and put my head down. Who would want to kill me? And who escaped the fight at Proctor House? I couldn't think of anyone. It was amazing how quickly my sense of peace could be destroyed. "I can't think of anyone."

"Steve, can we . . . sweep him up?" my mother asked.

He nodded. "Try to get all of him, and put him in a clean plastic bag just in case we need any forensic tests."

"Detective, this is all my fault. For months I've been here every night, keeping the apothecary safe. Now that I've moved back to Proctor House, suddenly it's not safe here," my father said.

My mother brought out the dust pan and broom and began to sweep up the ashes of the man who had the unfortunate timing to set off the spell. If he'd been a minute earlier or later, he might still be alive. Then a thought hit me. What if one of my clients had come in at ten? What if Mrs. Williams wanted her tea first thing this morning? What if a new customer never even made it into the shop?

My hands began to shake, and I could feel my stomach start to heave. I closed my eyes and forced myself to take slow, deep breaths.

"Isabella, are you okay?" my father asked.

I kept my eyes closed. "No. There's ginger in the prep room."

He was back in an instant and put a slice of candied ginger in my hand. I chewed it and let it settle my stomach. When I felt like I could control my stomach, I opened my eyes. Sevigny's ashes were gone and everyone was staring at me. "I'm okay now. I was just having a moment—what if one of my customers had been here at the wrong time? I could have been responsible for their death. In fact, I'm responsible for that man's death. How could I have not checked the building when I walked in this morning?"

The fact was, I didn't always check the building in the morning. I refreshed the wards at night, but I put too much faith in them to bother inspecting the shop in the morning.

My mother put her hand on my shoulder. "No one checked the building this morning. If anyone's to blame, it's me. I should know better."

"If the three of you are done taking responsibility for this man's death, can we talk about who is really responsible? The person who put the spell on the building? Who could have done that?"

I looked at my father. "Is there anyone left in the fraternity with enough power to cast that spell?"

He shrugged. "I'm not sure. I wasn't able to get to everyone I wanted during the fight. You don't have any other witch enemies, do you?"

I thought for a moment. I wasn't the favorite person for most people in the New Hampshire sorority, but I couldn't imagine any of them wanting to kill me. "No. Things are okay with the sorority, and I can't imagine anyone wanting to kill me."

"I need to call the chief," Palmer said. "Can I use your office?"

I nodded and handed him the key. It was unlike him to need privacy when we were working on a case together. What did he have to say that he didn't want us to hear?

After Palmer closed the door to my office, my father sighed. "Palmer doesn't trust me. I can't say that I blame him either."

I didn't understand. He'd been here for months protecting me and the shop, hadn't he earned Palmer's trust?

"Put yourself in his shoes. He's got a murder here, with three suspects standing around waiting for him to arrive. He knows it's not you, he's pretty sure it's not M, so that leaves me. Or some other person he has no idea how to find. On top of that, the only people who can tell him what's going on are the suspects, and it's unlikely that either of you would point the finger at me, not when I've only just come back into your lives."

I nodded. "So he has no idea what to do. No wonder he wants to confer in private. Aren't you worried?"

My father smiled. "No. I've known Ray for decades. We grew up together, and he knows I wouldn't kill someone. Even if he's suspicious, he knows I'd never involve my daughter or my wife."

Palmer left my office. "The chief is coming down. I'm not sure what to do about the case, but he assures me we can handle it in a way that looks non-magical."

My dad slapped Palmer on the back. "I've got to say, you're doing a great job dealing with all this magic. Most people freak out and run away."

I couldn't help but think about Thea's father. He ran away and never came back. A pang of guilt over having my father back hit me. Thea's father was gone and Delia's father . . . wait a minute. "Now that Forster has no power, can we break Delia's father free from the fraternity?"

My father looked to my mother. "I don't know. It's been a day already, and he hasn't made any moves to get in touch."

"Nadia hasn't said anything to me."

My heart sank. If he didn't take the opportunity to run, maybe he didn't want to. I'd just have to share my father as much as possible.

The chief walked into the shop and immediately focused on my father. He grinned and laughed. "Alex? Is that you?"

"In the flesh," my dad said.

They hugged and slapped each other on the back. "I can't believe you're back," the chief said. "Never thought I'd see you again."

They let each other go. "Wasn't sure I'd ever make it back. But you've done a fine job watching after my family. Thank you."

"You've got a great daughter—all from her mother, I'm sure. Isabella didn't take much work, at least not until she started helping out with our cases. She's got a talent for it, though. People naturally trust her and they'll open up to her, tell her the truth when they wouldn't dare talk to our officers so freely."

The ginger had finally fixed my stomach, and I was ready to get back to the investigation. "Sounds like the two of you need a man date to catch up. Can we get back to the dead man in my doorway?"

"Detective Palmer took photos, then I swept him up," my mother explained. "We were afraid someone might come in and see him."

"There was a spell on the door designed to kill the person who walked into the shop at exactly ten in the morning," my father said.

"This man opened the door and said he was Jason Sevigny, from the law firm Trina used. He stepped into the building and that's when he turned to ash. Instantaneously." Now that I thought about it, at least he hadn't suffered.

The chief pursed his lips. "Alex, you investigated the spell?"

"It was faint, so I needed M's help. It's gone now, no one would be able to tell it was ever there," my father said.

"Okay, so what happens tomorrow at ten?" Palmer asked.

My father frowned. "Nothing. That spell is gone, and I'm moving back here to protect the shop. No one will be able to do this again."

"But we just got you back," my mother said. "I'm going wherever you go from now on. I don't care if I have to freeze in a tent until it gets warm in the summer."

The chief looked at Palmer. "If Alex and Michelle say the spell is gone, it's gone. Obviously neither of them wanted to harm their daughter, so we need to look somewhere else for suspects. And we're going to ignore the missing man until someone reports him. He'll be an unsolved missing persons case until someone confesses."

I could tell by the look on Palmer's face he didn't like this idea. "We're playing it fast and loose with the truth here. His car is probably parked out front, and it's going to come back to Isabella sooner or later."

"Yes, it will. And the story is he never made it into the shop. It's as close to the truth as we can get, because I am not throwing my career away by explaining what happened. And neither are you."

Palmer took a minute to think. "That's fine for a civilian, but I've sworn an oath to uphold the law. I can't let the crime go uninvestigated, and I'm sure not going to let Isabella stay in danger for a minute longer than necessary."

Hosta la Vista

"Here's what's going to happen. Sooner or later, we're going to find the perp. Hopefully sooner. At that point, the sorority is going to take him off our hands, and we'll let their justice system deal with him. Justice will be served, and magic will still be a secret. Can you live with that?"

"Yes. But—"

"Listen, if we don't get any traction on this case in a few days, you can take some personal time and follow it up on your own, okay?" the chief asked.

Palmer looked a little relieved. "Okay. Two days."

"I'll find him before then," my father said.

"Let us do our job," the chief said. "You just got home, don't jeopardize time with your family. In fact, if you stay with them, keep them safe, we'll be able to get our job done a lot easier. Can you do that for me, Alex?"

He said yes, but I didn't believe him. Come to think of it, I wasn't sure I believed Palmer either. Those two were going to go off and do whatever they thought was right the minute the chief turned his back. And I wanted in on the action.

Chapter 19

The chief left and Palmer took another call in my office. When he finished the call, he said, "Jackpot!"

I looked at him, confused. "What do you mean?"

"Kate says our forensic accountant has found some issues with the Fancy Tart's accounts. We need to go talk to Shrewsbury and find out what he was doing."

I grinned. "Excellent. I want to keep my eye on him. He's never seemed trustworthy to me."

My father put his coat on. "I'm not hanging around here waiting for someone who doesn't know what they're looking for to stumble into a magical situation that could get them killed. I'm finding who wanted my daughter killed."

I wasn't used to hearing such anger, and the tone of his voice frightened me. "And bring him in for Hope to deal with, right? No vigilante justice."

He looked at me, sadness in his eyes. "We've got a lot of catching up to do, if you think I'd resort to that." He kissed my mother, then me, and disappeared.

Palmer shuddered. "It's going to take me a long time to get used to that. Can you come with me, or do you need to stay here?"

I looked at my mother. "Go. I'll run the shop for the day. But I'm going to ask for a raise when you get back," she said.

"How about a hundred percent raise?" I asked, laughing.

As we drove the few blocks to the lawyer's office, Palmer chuckled. "You don't pay her anything, do you?"

"I don't. But I should buy her a nice gift for all the time she's spent working for me." What would my mother want, anyway? I didn't recall her ever wishing for something she didn't wind up getting for herself. And now that my father was home, or at least in town, I doubted she wanted anything at all.

"Maybe a winter sleeping bag. If she's really going to stay out back with your father, she'll need it," Palmer suggested.

I thought about that for a minute. My father never looked like he was suffering in the cold. "She won't. I think he's got all sorts of spells set up in the tent. It's probably warm, dry, and bigger on the inside. Bats, he could have enchanted the tent to be larger than my apartment if he wanted to."

Palmer parked and stared at me. "He could? So all the pity I felt for him was wasted, and he could be living more comfortably than either of us?"

I nodded. "The more I think about it, the more likely I think it's true. We should ask for a tour."

"Could you do that to your apartment? Make it bigger?" he asked.

I'd never considered making the apartment bigger. Maybe because when I first moved out, I had a roommate who would have freaked out if she knew I was a witch. Also, we never needed to enlarge Proctor House, not even when we were kids. "I could," I said slowly, "but anyone coming into the apartment would notice. I'm not sure how I'd have explained that to Abby, or my landlord. It's easier to do when you can control who comes in."

"Ready?" he asked.

The door to the lawyer's office opened and Shrewsbury stuck his head out. He saw Palmer and me, and rushed back into the building. "Shoot. Someone must have tipped him off. Let's go," Palmer said. "I'll get the back door, you make sure he doesn't leave by the front."

Palmer raced to the back of the building while I walked to the front, tripping spell ready. I didn't need to catch him, just hold him up until Palmer could capture him. I entered the building and stood by the door.

"Miss Proctor, so nice to see you again," the receptionist said. "Mr. Shrewsbury is in meetings all day. Perhaps he could call you back tomorrow."

"That won't be necessary. I'm sure Detective Palmer has him by now."

The receptionist paled.

"You might want to spend the rest of your day looking for a new job. I'm not sure he'll be in business much longer."

She reached under her desk, picked up her bag and found her car keys. "He's being arrested? And he'll go to jail?"

I wasn't sure about any of that. "All I know is that Detective Palmer wants to talk to him. I'm not sure I can say anything else."

She rushed out and, through the open door, I saw Palmer with his hand on Shrewsbury's shoulder.

When I joined them, I noticed Palmer hadn't used his handcuffs. "You coming along with us, or do I need to call a patrol car and use handcuffs?"

Shrewsbury's eyes widened. "No need for any of that. Let's keep this civil and avoid tarnishing my reputation."

Palmer scoffed. "Let's go."

Shrewsbury's lawyer met us at the police department. He made a show of greeting us, shaking hands, and smiling. From the outside, you'd never know his client was a murder suspect.

We got settled into the interrogation room, and Palmer surprised me by handing the interrogation over to me. "I'd like my associate to begin the questioning, if you don't mind."

Russ DeLuca looked at me, and it was obvious he thought I was too young to be an effective interrogator. "Of course. What is this, a work–study program?"

I smiled, trying to look a little unsure of myself. "Tell me, Mr. Shrewsbury, can you explain the irregularities in Mrs. Swift's business accounts?"

He looked to his lawyer, who nodded. "No, I can't. I'd need to see the books. But I can assure you that there are no irregularities. Perhaps you are not reading them correctly? Understandable in someone so young."

As if on cue, Papatonis knocked and walked in with a file box. "Here's the paperwork you asked for, boss."

Palmer smiled. "Thanks."

Papatonis left and Palmer handed me a folder from the box labeled October POS. I opened it, keeping the pages upright so neither lawyer across the table from me could read them. The first page was the report from Bethany's point-of-sale machine. The second was the lawyer's report on her income. The lawyer's report was a thousand dollars lower. I replaced the folder and chose another at random. Again, there was a discrepancy of a thousand dollars.

"Look at this," Palmer said, handing me a folder labeled October credit card. As I flipped through the statement, I saw charges I couldn't believe were Bethany's, including a weekend's worth of charges from Antigua. Bethany hadn't taken more than an afternoon off in all the time I knew her, and she certainly wouldn't jet off to a tropical island for a weekend.

DeLuca cleared his throat. "If you need more time to do your homework, we can return tomorrow."

I set the file down. "That won't be necessary. I'd like to see his passport."

"That's not covered in the warrant," DeLuca said.

"I'm sure we can clear this all up with a minimum of fuss once we get a quick look at your client's passport," Palmer said. "Or we can wait right here for a judge to issue another warrant. It's up to you."

The two lawyers whispered to each other. I was surprised they didn't ask to speak alone.

Finally, DeLuca said, "I'll have his wife bring it."

While DeLuca was outside calling Shrewsbury's wife, I continued to ask questions. "We have files now, and they seem to all have financial discrepancies. Would you like to choose one at random to look through?"

"I'm not answering anything until my lawyer returns," he said.

I reopened the file in front of me. "According to this credit card statement, someone had a weekend in Antigua. We both know Bethany didn't take vacations. Were you on vacation? These charges look like you brought someone with you. Perhaps your wife? We can ask her when she gets here."

"No comment," was all he had to say.

I started reading through the files. I wanted to separate them into months with embezzlement and months without. The first five files all went into the embezzlement pile. "I'm reading through each of these files while we wait for your passport. I'm separating them into files with financial misconduct, and files without. You can see there's only one group of files. Care to guess which they are?"

"No comment," he said.

Palmer sat still and stared at the anxious Shrewsbury. He could watch me as I read through the files that proved his guilt, he could stare back at Palmer, or he could look at himself in the one-way mirror.

I finished examining the files and every single one showed signs of embezzlement. In fact, he grew bolder as time went on. I wasn't even sure how Bethany was able to keep the

Fancy Tart afloat. "I can't wait to see her personal finances too."

"You can't—No comment."

I returned the files to the box and placed the box under the table. "I hardly think I need to tell you this, but since you're not under arrest you can tell us anything you like. If there are extenuating circumstances, now is the time to let us know. Maybe we can help you."

"No comment."

I was disgusted. "So you thought you'd steal from Bethany? How did that seem okay to you? Don't you have any ethics?"

DeLuca walked in holding an open passport. "This should be all that you need."

Palmer took the passport and flipped through it to the front pages. "It's expired. Where's his current one?"

I felt like an idiot for asking Shrewsbury about his ethics. If his lawyer was trying to pass off an expired passport, it was likely neither of them had much of a moral compass.

Reluctantly, DeLuca pulled another passport out of his suit pocket. "I must have handed you the wrong one. Here's his current passport."

Palmer flipped through the pages, stopping when he got to an Antigua stamp.

Shrewsbury bit his lip. "You don't know how hard it is."

I had no idea how hard it was to be a lawyer. But I certainly knew how hard it was to be a struggling merchant. I looked at him with as much sympathy as I could muster. "No, I don't. Why don't you tell me?"

He looked to the door, then back to me. "It's my father-in-law. He's relentless."

DeLuca put his hand on his client's arm. "You don't need to say anything."

"But I'm not going to be arrested for murder. I want to make a deal."

"Deal? You're about to admit to a crime, and you can't implicate any of your clients, so what can you tell me that's of any use?" Palmer asked.

"I . . . I've got friends who don't always stay on the right side of the law," Shrewsbury stuttered.

"Don't," his lawyer advised.

"But I'll need protection. Some of these guys, they'd shoot you first and ask questions later."

"I doubt I can provide any protection. Why don't you start at the beginning and tell me why you put your practice at risk. By all accounts, you're successful—why risk it all?" Palmer asked.

Shrewsbury bit his lip again and looked toward DeLuca. DeLuca shook his head.

"I've got to give them something. It's only a matter of time before he follows the money back to me," he said as he gestured to Palmer. He sat up straighter and began to tell his story. "My father-in-law is always on at me about how he took his wife on vacations whenever she asked, because he worked so hard making money, taking care of the house and the children. He always had a new car. He never sent his children to public school." Shrewsbury sighed. "He has no idea how hard it was to keep up with all of that spending. I did it by borrowing every penny I could, and now I've got to pay it back. The business just isn't making enough for me to keep up with the payments anymore."

DeLuca sighed, then leaned over to whisper into Shrewsbury's ear, only this time he didn't bother to be so quiet. "If you're going to confess to a crime, there's not much I can do to help you. If you don't want my help, I can go."

Palmer stood and commanded Shrewsbury to do the same. "I'm arresting you for embezzling funds from the Fancy Tart and Bethany Swift."

Palmer continued to read him his rights as DeLuca and I stood up too. When Palmer had finished, I said, "One more question. Did you kill Bethany?"

Shrewsbury looked appalled. "Of course I didn't. The risk that her heirs would have her books examined closely was too great."

The three men walked out of the interrogation room, leaving me to think about what Shrewsbury said. His response made sense, unless Bethany called him before anyone else to talk about the discrepancies in her books.

Chapter 20

We left the interrogation room and I felt unfulfilled. Yes, we'd caught someone who'd been taking advantage of Bethany—and most likely Trina, now that I thought about it—but I didn't think he murdered Bethany.

"If that's all you've got for me today, I'd really like to get back to the apothecary. My mother's been stuck there for days now."

He stopped walking. "I know you said no lunch together, but I skipped breakfast. Can we just grab breakfast and talk over the case? After that I'll drive you wherever you want to go."

Hosta la Vista

I ought to get myself a car. I was getting tired of relying on other people for a ride, and I didn't think I was ready to teleport myself anywhere. Jameson didn't think I'd ever learn. "Okay, but not a café. I'm not ready to replace the Fancy Tart yet."

"Crispy Biscuit? I could use some eggs," Palmer suggested.

That was perfect. I could walk to the apothecary from there.

Once we got into the car, he started to ask me questions. "Are you seeing that guy again?"

I rolled my eyes. "Liam? Yes. Once we find Bethany's killer, we've got plans to go out."

He stopped at a red light. "Oh. I'm not sure he's the right guy for you."

It was obvious that Palmer regretted saying he wouldn't date me anymore but, so far, he hadn't said it. And as much as I liked Liam and found him comfortable to be around, working with Palmer again proved that we belonged together—personally and professionally. But he broke up with me, and he needed to work for it if he wanted to get back together. "What makes you say that?"

The light turned green and he turned left. "I just think you'd be better off with someone else."

I tried not to grin. We both knew who he was talking about. "Really?"

He parked a block away from the Biscuit. "Yes. Really. You need someone to challenge you, not just fit seamlessly into your world. You'll get bored with him—trust me."

I thought about what he said as we walked to breakfast. Would I get bored with Liam? Did I want to be challenged by my partner? And could I have both men in my life—Palmer could be my professional, challenging partner and Liam could be my personal, non-challenging partner.

I shook my head. No. I didn't like that idea at all. But I didn't know what to do. "I don't know about that. Can we just stick to the case?"

He opened the door to the Biscuit. I hadn't gone back since Emma died, and it was time I did.

Our waitress sat us at a booth by the window. "Can I start you off with something to drink?"

"Coffee for me," Palmer said.

I didn't want coffee from here. I wanted coffee and a croissant from the Fancy Tart. I bit my lip to keep tears from spilling out. The Tart was an integral part of the town, and I was sure it would be rebuilt. Sure, it might have a different owner and a different name, but it would always be the Tart to me. "Hot cocoa, please."

"Sure thing, honey," she said as she departed.

Palmer reached his hand out to me and, without thinking, I took it. "You okay?" he asked.

I nodded. "Just a minute of sadness. I'd rather be at Bethany's, you know?"

He squeezed my hand. "Yeah, I do."

I took my hand out of his. What was I thinking? "Let's talk suspects."

Our waitress brought drinks and we each ordered eggs and bacon. "Omar is out."

Palmer added cream and sugar to his coffee. "I agree. As angry as he might have been at her, he doesn't have it in him to kill anyone. I wouldn't have let you hire him if he did."

I couldn't believe I'd heard him correctly. "Do you want to rephrase that?"

He flushed. "Yes. As soon as I said it, I knew it came out wrong. If I thought he was a credible suspect, I would have strongly urged you not to hire him."

I raised an eyebrow.

"Of course, it's your business and you've proved to yourself and everyone else that you know what you're doing over the past year."

I smiled at him. It was nice to hear he and other people thought I knew what I was doing. I'd remember that for the next time I had a crisis of confidence. "Thank you. But if you thought I was putting myself in danger, I'd want to hear about it. I might not take your advice, but I'd at least consider what you had to say."

I took a sip of my hot cocoa, enjoying the fact we were having another pleasant conversation. I could get used to this. I wanted to get used to this, but I didn't dare. "Okay, so if Omar isn't a suspect, who have we got?"

He winced. "I'm not convinced we have anyone. Omar doesn't have it in him. Shrewsbury . . . he had the ring of truth when he said he wouldn't kill her because his books wouldn't withstand the scrutiny. And Andrew? He's the closest we've got. Even though he doesn't seem particularly sad she's gone, my gut says it's not him."

"Okay, then where else can we look?" I thought for a moment. "How about the other arsons? Maybe this didn't have anything to do with Bethany, and she was just an innocent victim?"

Our waitress brought our breakfast and we both started eating. After a few bites, Palmer said, "I don't know. I looked through those files, but couldn't make a direct connection between the fire at the Fancy Tart and any of the others. We need to widen our scope and start looking at other people we dismissed out of hand."

I finished off a strip of bacon. "Like who?"

"That's just it, I don't recall writing anybody off right away. That's not what we do. Maybe we were wrong to ignore the romance angle. Just because she was older doesn't mean she wasn't seeing anyone."

I stifled a laugh. I couldn't see Bethany dating anyone. She was married to the café and never spoke about anyone outside of her work life. "I doubt it. Have you gone through her house? Any evidence of a romantic partner?"

"I did, but no luck. Kate said she felt sorry for her, because it looked like there was no one else in her life except people from work."

My heart ached for her. I'd never considered asking her to go anywhere with me, just because we weren't the same age. And now I felt like I'd neglected a friend for the foolish idea that people were only friends with others their own age. "I never thought to ask her out for lunch, or have her over to my apartment."

Palmer reached across the table and took my hand. "It's not your fault. She always seemed busy, and had she ever invited you to go anywhere with her?"

I shook my head, giving me time to swallow the food in my mouth. "No. I never saw her outside of the bakery or the apothecary."

Something out the window caught my eye. I turned and saw bright flashes of magic on the sidewalk across the street, some coming from my father, and some coming from a man I'd never seen before. There was also a haze of magic covering the entire street and both sidewalks, keeping people from walking or driving near them. My father was trying to keep civilians safe.

"Hey, that's my dad outside. I'm going to check on him. I'll be right back."

Palmer looked behind him, out the window. "Is he . . . fighting with someone?"

I nodded as I stood.

"I'm coming with you," he said.

I held my hand out. "No. Let us handle it for now. You can make the arrest once it's safe."

He stood as though he was going to ignore my instructions. I suspected the haze would keep Palmer from actually coming outside, but I didn't want to risk it.

"Please. Your amulet may not fully protect you if you get in their way, and I don't want to split my focus by having to worry about you. I'll let you know when to come out."

As I got closer to the door, I was amazed at how much I wanted to stay inside. My father's spell was stronger than I'd expected it would be. I forced myself through the Crispy Biscuit's door and stood with my back against the building. I didn't want to get caught by the spells these men were hurling at each other. My hand reached out for the door to go back inside before I realized what I was doing. I pulled it down and grasped my amulet. *Help me stay out here*, I begged it.

The two men looked evenly matched and I wasn't sure how I could help. I didn't want to ask because, if I pulled my father's attention from the fight, he might lose. But if I cast any but the weakest spells, I might draw his opponent's attention, and I was sure I couldn't fight him off, not even with the amulet.

I cast an invisibility spell over myself and walked past the two men. Once I was behind my father's opponent, I crossed the street and prepared a binding spell in my mind. Jameson had finally taught me the spell Eunice used to pin me to the ceiling of Proctor House a while ago. It was the strongest binding I knew and, while I knew it wouldn't hold this man for long, it might be enough to give my father the upper hand. I added a small improvement, making the bindings invisible in case anyone was watching from inside.

To give myself the upper hand, I stuck my foot out. As our opponent fell, I cast my binding spell. Once I had him bound to the sidewalk, I ran toward my father. *Get him quick, Dad!*

He didn't need me to tell him what to do, but I wanted him to know I was here so that if he needed more help, he could call on me.

"Get back inside, Isabella," my father said in a harsh whisper. "It's too dangerous for you out here."

I wanted to stay outside, but he'd strengthened the hazy spell around me, and I couldn't fight off the need to go inside. I turned and ran back to the Crispy Biscuit, barely remembering to drop my invisibility spell before I went back inside. Palmer was standing at the window, watching the two men.

"What's going on out there?" Palmer asked.

Hosta la Vista

"You can't see it," I whispered, "but there's a lot of powerful magic going on out there." My father drew closer to his opponent and when he touched the man on the ground, black smoke ran from him, through my father, and into the road. After a full minute, the man stopped fighting and my father staggered, almost falling to his knees.

The red haze lifted and I grabbed Palmer's hand. "Let's go."

We rushed outside. I supported my father and Palmer helped the other man up. "What's going on here?" Palmer asked.

"This is Hector Bracken," my father said. "He's the one who set the trap on Isabella's door, and who set fire to the Fancy Tart."

Palmer didn't arrest people just because someone told him to. When Palmer didn't immediately put Bracken in handcuffs, he tried to run, but only got a few steps away because he was as exhausted as my father. "Not so fast. I think we'll all go to the station and get to the bottom of this."

Palmer radioed ahead and the chief was waiting for us in the parking lot.

The minute we got out of the car, the chief was giving orders. "Palmer, get that man into an interrogation room, then meet me in my office. Isabella, you and Alex come with me."

We followed the chief into his office. He shut the door and started to laugh. For twenty years I never thought I'd see you again, thought you were probably dead, and here we are twice in one day. Hey, I wanted to ask you earlier, any news about Calvin? Is he going to suddenly show up here too?" Why would the chief want to know about Delia's father? How did he even know Calvin's name?

We all sat and my father shook his head slowly. "Calvin is . . . not good. I'm not sure he'll ever be right again. He hasn't tried to make contact."

The chief leaned forward. "I can't accept that. All three of us should be here."

The three of us? "Hey, wait a minute," I said, taking my time to think. "Are you saying that you're . . ." I couldn't finish my thought. It was so preposterous, but also so right.

The chief sighed. "Please let me tell her."

I wasn't sure I could keep this big a secret from Thea. "Right now, let's go. There's no way I can look her in the eye and not tell her that you're her father."

Palmer knocked on the door and walked in. "Bracken's in room two. He's agitated and I've got Papatonis watching him."

The chief wiped his eyes. "Good. Now that you're here, Alex can tell us what was going on."

My father stood and paced the office. "You know about the fraternity?"

The chief nodded. He didn't look happy to be talking about them. "We've had some of them through here."

"The good news is that two nights ago we caught most of them as they were attacking Proctor House." My father paused for the chief to process that.

"Why didn't I hear anything about this? Why didn't the neighbors . . . Oh. Never mind." He looked at me. "Is everyone okay?"

I smiled. "Yes, we're all fine. My father's exhausted and shouldn't be out hunting down the last of the fraternity on his own, but we'll keep an eye on him from now on. Hope sent them to Sewall for trial."

My father shot me a disapproving look. "I was not hunting them all down. For your information, he attacked me."

The chief looked at Palmer. "Did you see what happened? Is this true?"

My father turned to glare at the chief. "I can't believe you'd ask that, Ray. Have I ever lied to you?"

Palmer looked at me, and I shrugged. These two were going to have to work out their relationship now that my father was back in town. "I don't know. Isabella noticed them first, and I couldn't tell what was going on between them."

The chief looked at me. I wanted to back up my father's story, but I really didn't know how it started. "They were already fighting when I looked out the window."

"He said next time he'd make sure the spell hit Isabella and not some random person walking through the door," my father said. "I couldn't just let him walk away."

The chief pursed his lips. "No, I suppose you couldn't. But would it kill you to call me for some help?"

My father's brows furrowed in anger. "Yes. It might. If I have to worry about defending you and fighting someone else, especially as strong as he was, someone could get hurt."

Palmer interrupted what was about to become an argument. "So you want me to question him about Sevigny's death. Did he confess anything else to you?"

My father sat, and only then did I notice how exhausted he was. He didn't look this tired a half an hour ago. I needed to get him home. "He said Forster told him to ruin Isabella's life. He started with the bakery, then moved on to the apothecary." He took my hand. "That's why I had to take his magical abilities away. I didn't want to, but he was out to kill you."

I squeezed his hand. That must have been the black smoke I saw moving from Bracken, through my father, and into the pavement. "It's okay, Dad. Let's get you home and I'll fix you up with another one of those restoration potions."

He shuddered. "Only one. I don't care how many your mother tries to give me. One potion and a long nap and I'll be fine."

I wasn't sure I believed him, but we could always start with just one potion. If he needed more, I was sure my mother and grandmother would find a way to get it in him.

Chapter 21

By the time we got my father home, I was still reeling from the bombshell the chief had dropped. He was my uncle, Thea's father. No wonder he was always looking out for me and my cousins. I thought he just had a crush on Aunt Lily. I never thought he'd have run away from a difficult situation. On the other hand, he was a different person now than he had been twenty-one years ago.

Palmer stayed to interrogate Bracken while the chief, or Uncle Ray, drove my father and me back to Proctor House. We each took one arm and helped my father into the house. He sat at the table and I went off to find my mother. I didn't have to go far, because she was rushing to the kitchen. "Where is he?" she asked.

"In the kitchen. He needs one of those disgusting potions, because he had a fight with one of Forster's men," I said.

My mother rushed past me, and I followed. "You foolish, foolish man! What were you thinking?"

I recognized her tone and knew she could go on for quite a while when she was this upset. She stopped when she realized he wasn't listening. I reached into the fridge, pulled out a potion and handed it to her.

She changed her tone and softly called his name. "Alex, it's time for your potion."

He closed his lips and turned his head away, like a child who didn't want to take his medicine. But then he turned back to her. "Okay, let's get it over with. Give it to me."

Hosta la Vista

I felt sorry for him as I poured a glass of milk.

He took the potion, uncorked the bottle and drank it like it was a shot of liquor. "Milk," he groaned. I handed him the glass. He didn't drink the milk nearly as fast. He swished some of it around his mouth as though trying to get every part of the potion and its foul taste away from his taste buds. He gargled a little more, then drank the rest.

The chief looked worried. "Is he going to be okay?"

My mother smiled. "He'll be fine tomorrow, or maybe the next day. But for now he needs to go upstairs and sleep."

My father looked like he wanted to argue, but he let out a huge yawn instead. "Fine. I'll nap, but you need to wake me up when the girls get back from work."

"Of course. Let's get you upstairs," she said as she lifted him out of the chair. She waited until only I could see her, then teleported him upstairs.

The chief looked nervous. "I guess I should speak to Lily, let her know you figured out who I am."

I sat at the table. I had a few questions I wanted to ask him while we were alone. If I waited until everyone was home, I'd never get a word in edgewise. "Can we talk for a minute first?"

He sat, still looking wary, and didn't say anything.

I closed my eyes and collected my thoughts. "Were you ever going to tell us who you were? Or were you going to let Thea think she'd been abandoned her whole life?"

He cleared his throat. "Well, ah, at first I wanted nothing to do with your family. I'm ashamed of my actions, but I've tried to make up for them, while respecting your family's wishes, for a long time now."

Aunt Lily opened the kitchen door, felt the mood of the room, and said, "What's wrong?" She closed the door, put her shopping bag on the counter and stared at the two of us. It turned out neither of us could keep a secret for long when she was staring at us.

The chief said, "Isabella knows," as I started to say, "I know who he is."

Aunt Lily hung her coat by the door and reached into the cabinet Grandma kept her whiskey in. She took out a glass, then looked back at us. I shook my head, but the chief nodded. "Just a little."

When she'd poured the whiskey and sat down, she took a deep breath. "Twenty-one years we've kept this secret. What happened today that suddenly you had to tell her?"

She sounded angry, and as much as I was upset, too, it wasn't completely his fault. "I was starting to guess when he and my father were talking. Then when he started asking about Delia's father, it just all seemed to click."

Aunt Lily drank half the finger of whiskey she'd poured for herself. "You know Isabella's not going to be able to keep this a secret for very long, right?" She turned to me. "I could erase your memory, if you'd let me."

I didn't like that idea at all. "If I put it together once, I'll figure it out again, sooner or later. Then we'd have to go through the whole memory erasure again, and that's assuming I don't figure it out and immediately tell her. I think we should be honest and get it all out into the open."

I could tell Aunt Lily didn't like my idea, but there was no way she'd argue against being honest. "What about Delia?" she asked.

"I'm sure Alex can tell her things about him. Maybe he could tell her a nice story so she wouldn't feel so bad?" I suggested.

Aunt Lily scoffed. "From what I've heard, there's nothing good to tell anymore. He's in the clutches of the fraternity, and they're never letting him go."

I thought for a minute. "But who's left? There can't be many with much power. Not after today, when Alex took Bracken's magic from him." I realized I hadn't filled anyone in on my morning. "We really need to have a family meeting."

Grandma walked into the kitchen. "What's going on here? Lily, is that my whiskey?" She looked from Aunt Lily to the chief, then to me. I couldn't keep the grin off my face. "Oh, bats. The secret's out." She poured herself a glass of whiskey and sat next to me. "You're right, we all need to talk."

We decided to give my father the day to sleep and have the meeting once Thea and Delia got home from work.

During the day, I finally made up my mind. I couldn't keep seeing Liam, not when

Palmer and I were well on our way to reconciling. Liam ticked all the boxes on the perfect boyfriend list: respectful, thoughtful, polite, interested in my work. And I had no doubt he'd make someone a fantastic husband. But I couldn't be that someone.

Palmer joined us when we were ready to meet because he needed to fill us in on Bracken's confession.

Thea and Delia opened the kitchen door and stopped in their tracks. "What's going on?" Delia asked, scanning the room. "Everyone's here, so no one's hurt. Is this about Grandma moving to that island?"

I'd forgotten about Grandma's plan to move.

"That's on hold for now. Come in, girls. We've got to talk," Grandma said.

The kitchen was too crowded, so we all moved to the blue dining room where Aunt Nadia had set out pizza for dinner. Ten people could eat a lot of pizza, and the table and

Hosta la Vista

sideboard were covered with different sizes, styles, and toppings. I took two slices of mushroom, pepper, and onion, thinking I'd go back for a slice of the prosciutto, mozzarella, and basil later.

When we were all seated, Aunt Lily started to speak. "It's about time we told you girls some things about your fathers. Now that Alex is here, and you're old enough to know the truth, we want you to know what happened when you were small." She looked at my mother and Aunt Nadia. "I'll go first. Thea, we told you that your father abandoned me when he found out I was a witch. That's true. But what we didn't tell you is that he had a change of heart and has been doing his best to watch over the entire family."

I couldn't help but look at the chief. He had tears in his eyes and a hopeful look on his face. *Please, Brigid, don't let her reject him.*

"What? No one's been looking after us. We've been on our own . . . except . . ." She looked at the chief. "No way! Is that why you always helped me whenever I called you?"

He nodded, unable to speak, but giving her a nervous smile.

Just when I thought I couldn't take the tension for a moment longer, the chief stood up. "I've done everything I could while respecting your mother's wishes. I'm not the man I was when I rejected you, and I hope that someday you'll—"

He didn't get to finish what he was saying because she rushed to him, hugging him as tightly as she could. When they started crying, the rest of the room joined them.

Aunt Nadia put her arm around Delia. Once we'd all dried our eyes, she said, "I'm not sure what to tell you about your father. When we were together, he was a good man and he loved you very much. He left after Alex, when they were both being pursued by the fraternity."

My father, who had been sitting quietly and barely looked awake, lifted his head to look at Delia. "For a while, we were together, but somehow he got caught. He begged me to escape, and I did. I went back for him a dozen times over the years, but I could never get to him. I'm so sorry, honey."

"Was he here at the house two nights ago? Is he in Sewall now? I want to go see him," Delia said.

"No, he wasn't. I looked but he wasn't here. Maybe it was too much for him to attack the house his family lived in. I won't stop looking for him, though."

Delia put her head on her mother's shoulder. My heart broke and I started crying for her. Of the three of us, she was the only one who hadn't met her father.

Palmer handed me a tissue. I looked up at him and tried to smile. He leaned in a little while he gently squeezed my shoulder. "Between the three of us, we'll find him." After a nod from the chief, Palmer turned to the rest of the family. "I've also got news about the fire at the Fancy

Tart, and the man who was incinerated at the apothecary."

My family went through another round of nose blowing and wiping tears away before he continued. "He's been arrested and has confessed to both crimes. Hope will pick him up in the morning. Thanks to Alex, he's got no powers and he won't be able to incinerate anyone again."

I was confused. "But why did he kill Bethany?"

"Forster told him to start hurting the people around you, to play with you and make you afraid for the lives of everyone you loved. He claims he only wanted to hurt her, but that doesn't matter. He'll spend the rest of his life in jail for the murders, and we'll never have to worry about him again. In fact, according to Hope, the fraternity is just about finished. Forster brought every witch he could find with any strong power. When you swept them all up and brought them to Sewall, you left only the weak and frightened witches, and my guess is that they'll never regroup."

I wasn't sure that was true. It only took one person to decide they wanted power over everything else to start up something like the fraternity again. But at least this time they'd be starting with much weaker witches. "The sorority will keep tabs on them, just to make sure."

Palmer bent down and whispered in my ear. "Can we go somewhere to talk?"

I nodded and led him to the living room. It wasn't private, but I wanted to keep my ear on what else might happen in the dining room.

He sat on the couch, then stood. He walked to the fireplace and stared into the mirror above it. Finally he turned to face me. "I was wrong."

I bit back the urge to ask what he was wrong about this time and just raised an eyebrow.

"Earlier today. Our roles were reversed. There was danger that only you could handle. You told me to stay where I was and not come out." He ran his hand through his hair. "And I did not like that. I'm the cop, I'm the one charged with keeping the peace, but I couldn't even tell anything was wrong. You were protecting me and making sure I didn't get hurt."

I nodded, but still said nothing.

"And now I know how you feel when I tell you to stay back. And how arrogant am I to assume that I can handle magical danger as well as you can? I'm sorry. But you've got to believe that all I want is to keep you safe."

"Same here. If they'd have noticed you out there, your amulet wouldn't have saved you. Mine barely kept me from running back into the restaurant. When I rush headlong into danger, it's so you'll be safe, behind me."

He sat next to me. "I understand. I can teach you how to shoot a gun, or any million other ways to defend yourself, but my instinct is always going to be to protect you."

"Like I said, it's the same for me. But I can't teach you magic. The only thing I can do is stand in front of you and keep you safe. As much as it might bruise your ego, you're the more vulnerable person here. And you've already shown that you can't live with that. So while I appreciate your apology, I don't think this leaves us anywhere different."

He took my hand in his. "I think it does. For all the talk about how much I respected your abilities, I didn't consider that I was the weaker partner."

That seemed to be going a little too far. "I wouldn't say that. As you said, you've got skills I don't have. And we've got each other's back. It seems to me that's the basis for a strong partnership."

As he leaned in to kiss me, he whispered, "That's what I thought too."

Special Acknowledgements

Writing a series of books isn't always easy and I have a lot of people to thank.

As always, thank you to my husband – I'm grateful he's never suggested I get a "real job" instead of writing.

My fantastic editor, Kath, has saved me from so many errors and confusing paragraphs and I absolutely could not have done any of this without her.

My cover designer, Karen, is a dream to work with and can take the tiniest idea of a cover and turn it into the fantastic covers we see now.

My writer's group – Rona, Sara, Laura, and sometimes Trish – I would never have gotten here without you!

My family, all of whom have supported me even though I'm sure they've thought "Mom's got another crazy idea she's going to try. Let's see how *this* one goes."

Thanks to my intermittent assistants, Noam and Chantelle – your work has saved me hours of time and let me focus on writing books.

And, saving the best for last, my deepest thanks to everyone who has read to this page. Your support, reviews, and messages have meant the world to me. I save them all and on days when I thought I'd never get to this point I've pulled them out and let them inspire me.

But wait, there's more!

I may be done writing this series, but Thea and Delia will be getting their own series. I've also got some things planned for Isabella and Palmer in the future, so we're not done with magical Portsmouth.

Made in the USA
Middletown, DE
07 April 2023